M

Whose World Is This?

The

John

Simmons

Short

Fiction

Award

University of

Iowa Press

Iowa City

*Lee
Montgomery*

Whose World Is This?

University of Iowa Press, Iowa City 52242

www.uiowapress.org

These stories have appeared in the following publications:
"What about That Thing, They Called," *Santa Monica
Review*; "We Americans," *Story*; "Whose World Is This?"
Iowa Review; "These Hours," *Black River Review*; "Arts and
Crafts of American WASPs," *Denver Quarterly*; "We the
Girly Girls from Massachusetts," *Antioch Review*.

The University of Iowa Press is a member of Green Press
Initiative and is committed to preserving natural resources.
Printed on acid-free paper

Library of Congress Cataloging-in-Publication Data
Montgomery, Lee (Lee Begole), 1957–
    Whose world is this? / by Lee Montgomery.
        p.   cm.—(The John Simmons short fiction award)
    ISBN-13: 978-1-58729-614-7 (pbk.)
    ISBN-10: 1-58729-614-4 (pbk.)
    I. Title.
    PS3613.O5488W47 2007   2007008810
    813'.6—dc22

07   08   09   10   11   P   5   4   3   2   1

for Tom, always

It's only the unknown

that shakes your poise.

—EMILY POST

Contents

ACKNOWLEDGMENTS

I am grateful to my sister, Lael, for her friendship and support from the very beginning. I would also like to again express thanks to my friends from Cleveland, Jim Krusoe and Angela Fasick, who have read my work ad nauseam and supported these stories in their earliest forms. A special appreciation goes to Anna Haude for the title and various other evidences of little girl brilliance. Big thanks to Anna Keesey and Ellen Fagg for critiques, laughs, and significant outfits. I am indebted to friends and mentors Deborah Eisenberg, Elizabeth Benedict, David Hamilton, Margot Livesy, and Connie Brothers for helping me along the way. Many thanks to Amy Hempel, the Iowa Writers' Workshop, John Simmons, and the University of Iowa Press. And, finally, I am grateful to the folks at *Tin House* for their friendship and support, with special thanks to Meg Storey, Holly MacArthur, CJ Evans, Emily Bliquez, and, last but not least, Win McCormack, whose generous support of contemporary literature and of those who write it makes the world a better place.

Whose World Is This?

Hats

A few days before my friend Christopher died,
he woke me up in the middle of the night and told me about all the
ladies in the drawers, and in the bathroom, and how they had to
leave before we could sleep. I got up and looked in the drawers and
told him that I couldn't see any ladies. I climbed into bed again.

"What about the bathroom?" he asked.

"They're sleeping."

"In the tub?"

"Yes."

We lay there for a long while looking at the ceiling.

"Do you think the fish up there are hungry?" he asked.

"They just had all that pizza," I said.

"Their sea is white," he said. "Who could imagine that and all the hats."

Then he laughed. "Fish in hats, just for the halibut," he said. "Oh, God! What's wrong with me?"

"You're queer, Christopher. You're queer."

A few years before, Christopher had told me he couldn't sleep at night because he was cold. He said he looked at his lover, next to him, wrapped up in the goose eiderdown they had purchased through a catalog, and wondered about it.

"I wanted to be under the covers," he said.

"Then why didn't you get under them?" I asked.

"Because I was in a box." He held up a clear plastic ruler with red lines on it. "I was in a shallow box the size of this ruler."

I looked at the ruler. It was only a foot long. Christopher was very big, about six feet long.

"I was in this box and I couldn't get under the covers," he said. "I was waiting for my drugs."

The day before, Christopher learned his blood cells were eating him alive.

The week before, he learned all about chemotherapy.

Three weeks before that, he learned about his cancer.

On the day he found out, I took him to lunch. We had made a deal. If he didn't have cancer, he took me out. If he did have cancer, I took him. That morning I found a note on my desk. "Looks like you owe me lunch, but now I get to eat whatever I want. I can eat all day."

We laughed because now he was doing chemo, he could eat anything and not get fat. I yelled about how unfair it was. He stared at me, dead-pan. "Don't hate me because I have cancer," he said.

That afternoon, we sat under an orange metal umbrella at a fake stone picnic table and talked about dying. We said things like, now that he may have only six months, what a helluva six months it would be.

He groaned slightly and told me about his new house, not so far from where we were sitting, maybe ten miles. He was moving in with his new lover, a man who worked in Hollywood and wore a big watch. He had just signed a one-year lease, and now he didn't know if he would live that long. Nevertheless, he said he dreamt of dinner parties on the deck and about all the decorations. "Now that I'm dying I'm going Nelly, queen all the way," he said. "Everything will have white pillars and be gold inlaid." He threw his head back dramatically the way a woman would. He also talked about wanting a dog. Now that he knew he was dying he was going to get a dog. "A dog will be good when I'm sick," he said. "I can hug him."

Christopher wanted to name the dog Ben, but he worried about it because he didn't want to die and leave the dog alone.

"Couldn't Jon take care of him?" I asked.

"Yeah, but I don't want him to have to look at the dog and be reminded of me."

We agreed that he should probably make out a will. I told him I wanted his convertible and the dog. He lay down on the bench and complained about the effort of it all and how he wished he didn't have to lose all his hair. He pulled at his eyebrows and his mustache and unbuttoned his shirt to feel the chest hairs. He said he had a fifty-fifty chance of living.

He was depressed also, he said, because he recently had lunch with a dear friend who was making a ton of money. "Did I tell you about my friend who is making $100,000 a year?" He would say this thirty times throughout the afternoon when we'd meet at the water fountain. I gave this a lot of thought, and at the twenty-fifth meeting I told him that life was not fair. I told him that when it rains in Bangladesh, people have to live in treetops. I told him also that I knew of people in Beverly Hills who had been promised free rent in the continuum. "These are the people who win Volvos and get to hear the chorus of angels when they go to Hawaii," I said.

Christopher told me then that he was going to max out all his credit cards and then declare bankruptcy. "If I'm going to die," he said, "maybe I could be rich before I go."

We were walking under a long line of fluorescent lights back to our office when he said it.

"Yeah," I answered. "And we could pack all the wads of money in your casket like King Tut."

"What about the gold?" he asked. "I want my dead body to be surrounded by gold."

"That's what I mean," I said. "And I'll put a ruby collar around your neck."

He stopped and looked at me then. The light in his eyes dimmed a little as if he had reached inside his head and turned the switch on one of those lamps that has three stops. When I saw that, I heard the click of the lamp that stood next to my father's favorite red leather chair. I could see his eyes closing and hear him say it was time to catch a little shut-eye.

Before my father died his eyes dimmed too. Little by little the light escaped until there was no more.

A month later, I was sitting in my office, a dull, somber place with no windows, when Christopher ran in, holding a handful of his hair. "It's coming," he said, throwing the hairs on my desk.

"Stop pulling it," I said.

"I'm pulling the gray out." He sat down across from me and pulled at his mustache and his eyebrows, throwing the hairs on my desk. I picked them up and threw them back at him. They fell through the air like snowflakes.

"Do you think I should do Phil Donahue or Liberace?" he asked.

He was talking about his wigs. He'd been brushing them and trying them on in front of the mirror for weeks. He told me that he was looking forward to losing his hair now, because he would be able to wear a lot of hats. We talked all about hats, and I told him that I thought he should wear a big floppy hat with a flurry of big red flowers packed on its brim. He said he would consider it, but what he really wanted was a hat like a gangster or, better yet, a cowboy. "Time to get my ass out of Dodge," he said, pretending to adjust his hat and pulling his mustache. A big clump of hair came out, and we both looked at it sandwiched between his fingers. I told him then that my husband was being transferred back to New York and we had planned to go in about a month.

"I think we'll be back in a few years," I said.

He said that not only would I miss the hats but also he'd be dead by then.

"Go ahead—miss the biggest event in my life," he said. "I'm going to die, and you're going to New York."

I told him that he couldn't die, that he was too young to die.

"I can't believe it. I'm dying, and you're going to New York," he said, pacing around the office, taking little steps, shoe to shoe, with his penny loafers.

"Christopher, you should really put some pennies in those loafers," I said.

"You're going to miss the whole hat chapter of my life," he said.

He yanked at both eyebrows at the same time and delivered two clumps of tiny hairs on my desk. His face looked all lopsided, because he now had big bald spots on his eyebrows and his mustache from all the pulling.

What about
That Thing,
They Called

When they were young, shortly after they had
fallen out of love but before they pulled apart for good and moved
to different latitudes in California, he in the north and she in the
south, Hilary and Bob lay naked on the rooftop of a three-story
tenement house in the North End of Boston. They were spending the evening together drinking gin and tonics, having sex, and
snorting drugs. It had rained earlier, and although it was now past
dusk, the sky still had color and the air was cool. This was a welcome thing. For weeks the heat had hung its miserable head in the
streets like a jilted lover, forcing the city's pace to a sluggish sigh.

They lay apart, their bodies flat against the warm asphalt,
touching nothing together, not even their eyes, which gazed

indifferently at opposite corners of the sky. In the cool color of the near darkness Hilary saw patterns of light that she imagined would spawn stars later. She felt grateful. Sorry. Even though she knew where the stars would be, her brain was dull; she couldn't remember their names.

She rolled over onto her stomach, resting her chin on her folded hands, and stared mindlessly out over the city. Beyond them were the rooftops of single-family brownstones and other triple-decker tenement-style apartment buildings. She could see brick sides of buildings and windows, some lit, some not. Through them life appeared unreal, flat and dull, like a childhood game in a box. She couldn't distinguish details, only shadows of women moving in and out of window frames and doorways, making dinner as if life with men made any sense at all. She imagined these women calling their men and children for supper, planning elaborate weekends and summer barbecues in their minds while listening to their families pad up and down long hallways. She heard children giggling *thankyouthankyouthankyou* at high octaves while their midget feet pounded against tireless wooden planks.

A woman poked her head out a window and yelled, her voice echoing throughout the streets. "Mary," she called. "Mary!"

Hilary and Bob looked at each other for a second, but it was only a second before they turned away, sharing silence and breath and the stupid dreamy look of two people who had just had sex, the kind of sex people have when their love has soured yet who remain high on each other's physicality, high on drugs on a rooftop in a city. It wasn't even an hour before that that their sweaty bodies had feigned love, felt the opportunity of it while bumping and grinding against each other and the asphalt, heaving like old engines. Sucking. Spitting. Groaning. For the hell of it. For the fuck of it. For old time's sake.

Hilary rolled over, balancing her body on its side, facing him. The curve of her hip was lovely, even though in the past year she had grown much too thin. With every pound she lost she became crazier. But even crazy she was beautiful. This was the danger. In their six years of on-again, off-again he had memorized her long bones, her two chipped front teeth that formed an upside-down V, and the trails of her startled dark eyes searching. She had cut her hair a few weeks before, so now it lay close to her skull in dark clumps, lending a new sadness, along with everything else.

She whistled a few bars of an old love song and then grabbed one of her breasts, holding it tenderly in the palm of her right hand.

"You know," she whispered while poking a finger at the nipple, "when a woman has inverted nipples, it makes her look at the world differently."

Bob groaned and laughed, his chest heaving in waves of sound and breath pressed together.

"I'm serious," she said. "Nothing comes easy for a woman with inverted nipples, and I can't help but think it is a statement, some statement on my ability to love. Or be loved."

"Ah for Christ's sakes," Bob said. "Don't even start."

"I do believe that," Hilary whispered. "What I just said. I *believe* it."

Bob rolled away, his back facing her, and she gazed at his wild auburn curls that coiled around themselves and rested against the nape of his neck. She ran a finger around his broad shoulders and down the long muscles of his back, marveling at the shape of his body: a human funnel. She patted his bottom, making sharp slapping sounds. She had adored that bottom once, but now she felt something different. It wasn't adoration or love but rather the memory of something like it along with a strange ache, a restlessness that comes from being with too many men, of wanting and not wanting. She climbed over him and fell sideways, her body hanging off his torso, her weight balanced on him and the back of her right shoulder. She touched his face, gently moving her fingers clockwise along the perimeter, from his forehead to his chin. He closed his eyes. She licked his left eyelid, dragging her tongue across it, and then stopped.

"That is why I adored Nicholas so," she said. "He loved my breasts. I guess I'm a whore for that sort of thing."

"Don't talk to me about him, Hilary," he said. "You're humiliating yourself again."

"He did love my breasts," she said. "He told me that. He told me all he wanted to do was suck them out. I mean he knew, being a doctor and all, that it is not a bad thing, not an abnormal thing, but just a variation. Most people don't know that. I think this is significant, Bob, I mean it's an important thing in a man. That kind of understanding. Of understanding things that others don't."

"Ah Christ, Hilary. You're crazy. If you ask me, you've been doing too much speed."

"Probably," she said. "He loved me, I think."

"But he left anyway," he said.

"Yes," she whispered again. "He said it was unfortunate circumstances. The fact that I am, in the end, pregnant. I spent the money he sent on cosmetics. So there. Dr. Neunecker, Fat Pecker. That's what my mother calls him. Dr. Fat Pecker."

She laughed. She touched Bob's lips with her index finger and kissed him.

"You love me, don't you though? Tell me that. Tell me you love me still after all."

"I don't," he said.

A sadness fell over her face and a certain shame, he thought, as if she was pulled between emotions and couldn't find herself.

"You did," she said. "You did love me."

"I did," he said.

"But you don't anymore?" she asked.

"Not in that way."

"How is it that you can stop loving someone and still sleep with them?"

"Why don't you tell me?"

"But I love you."

He pushed out a breath and laughed.

"You're imagining things again," he said. "With love there's loyalty, and face it, Hil, you've never been the loyal sort."

He untangled himself from her body and sat up. She readjusted herself and laid herself out flat, not looking at him but at the sky.

"If you have," she said, "if you really have just stopped loving me, why do you always come back? If I've stopped loving you, why do I always let you?"

His lips moved as if he wanted to say something. She rolled over onto her stomach and struggled to her feet.

"Talk to me," she said.

"What do you want to talk about?" he asked.

"Dishonesty," she said. "You're not an honest man, but you know me well enough to know I find dishonesty attractive. That is why I give good head on rooftops, because it's a thrill to know you want me, probably even still dream about me, even though you're in love with someone else. Or is it that I give such good head and you don't have the guts to ask the same of women you apparently love?"

"Hilary, stop," he said.

She leaned over and grabbed her drink and walked to the edge of the roof and looked down. Below her she could see the corner market still open, and for an instant just the sight of it brought her inside it. She felt the cool air from the air-conditioning on high and saw the few shelves packed with foods in weird packages from foreign countries.

"What would you do if I jumped?" she asked. "Would you feel sad? Would you think you loved me after all?"

"You're drunk," he said. "And annoying." He stood, grabbed his pants, and pulled them on.

"You are the one who told me that I could give the best head in town, weren't you? Or was that someone else?" she smiled. "I forget."

"You don't need to do this," he said. "I should go."

"Imagine the nations women could move by the simple gesture of sucking dick. Maybe there'd be no more war." She hesitated and smiled, walking toward him. "Isn't it strange that what men love most, women despise? What men love is what women find most humiliating."

He grabbed his T-shirt and pulled it over his head.

She placed a hand on his crotch and rubbed slowly. "I don't want you to leave me alone," she whined. "You're supposed to stay with me. Besides, I don't know where you're going. Where does someone like you go when you feel like you do?"

"Home," he said, taking her hand away and holding it out in front of him. "People like me go home to get out of the line of fire. You're in one of your desperate moods."

"But I thought you wanted to mourn the departure of the German girl," she said. She pulled her hand away from him and, losing her balance, sat down abruptly, looking slightly stunned from the impact.

"I wonder why she left," Hilary said, looking up at him. "You know, I kind of liked her, even though she had a flat ass. It must have felt different for you, or did you imagine mine? 'And when she left, he made love to her ghostly ass.'"

"You're sick, Hilary, and I'm going home, leaving you to your little game of psychological warfare."

"Is that what it is?" she called to him as he disappeared down the steps at the far end of the roof. "Is that what you call this? Hey you! Leave the drugs!"

"Have it your way," she said to no one a few moments later. She leaned back on her hands and stretched her legs out in front of her. She crossed them and uncrossed them for a few moments and watched the muscles strain. She then lay back, closed her eyes, and studied the darkness that came to her in colors. She felt swallowed by indigo blue.

―――――――――

When Bob had called Hilary earlier that evening to tell her that his new girlfriend from Germany had run off with his kung fu teacher, Hilary had laughed. She had laughed so hard that the pain in her stomach had started again.

"This is insane," she said. "I'm crawling around my apartment with this pain. It is really horrible, and all you can talk about is your flat-assed German girlfriend. I think I'm dying."

"That's what I like about you, Hilary, it's never serious," he said.

"It is. Serious."

Bob knew the history. Over the past few weeks two doctors had told Hilary that she was pregnant, but yesterday she was told she had a tumor. So beyond being afraid now that she was going to die, she was confused as to why.

"If I am going to die, at least I want to know why."

She fell silent for a moment.

"You're not dying," he said. "You're pregnant."

"Anything's possible," she said. "What I want to know, though, if I feel like I'm dying, how can you tell me I'm not? Why do you feel you can tell me what my reality is and is not?"

"Hilary," Bob said.

"I am dying," she yelled. "I am dying from immorality. Is that a word? I am dying from freedom."

"Hilary!" he said. "For Christ's sakes, you're not dying!"

"How would you know if I'm dying or not?" she said. "You don't know. I *could* die. There's nothing saying I won't, and my hope is, my real hope is that when I die you feel hideous, so hideous and sinful you would have to die too. You should feel really shitty about the German, leaving me for the German. That's what I'm dying of. Sadness, Bob."

"What are you talking about?" he said. "You left me."

"Given the circumstances of you and what's her face, what did you expect me to do?" she asked. "What was her name?"

"I don't remember," he said.

"Laird," she said. "Take out the 'i' and what do you get?"

Later, when Bob sat in the waiting room of the hospital in the middle of the night with Hilary's parents, who were looking old and worried after driving thirty miles in pouring-down rain, he thought about the insanity of that conversation, the insanity of all conversations with Hilary, really.

He looked around the white room with all the chairs lined up next to each other, seeing traces of Hilary in her parents' faces, and felt the likelihood of death for the first time, and what surprised him was that it felt smaller and more painful than he had imagined. Like a hole. He was leaking.

It was partly out of his suspicious nature, he told her parents, and partly out of fear that Hilary was right that he returned to the rooftop and found her lying facedown, her back silently taking on patterns of rain.

"She made no sound," he said. "Not a peep."

He turned and looked at the old man and his wife, their faces empty and haunted. They kept their London Fog raincoats on, pulled tightly around their round sagging bodies. The man tugged at his fingers, his hands pulling at each other on his lap. His wife knit a purple cable-knit sweater at a startling speed, needles clicking.

"Not a peep," Bob repeated.

Bob left the waiting room for a moment to get a cup of coffee. When he sat down again, he continued to talk about Hilary, telling the old man and woman how strong she was, how terribly spirited she was. He took a series of small breaths through his teeth as if he wanted to laugh as he told them how she had woken up in the emergency room and yelled at the doctor.

"She didn't even say hello," he said. "She said, 'Fuck you.'" And then Bob smiled a little as he took a breath and ran his finger along the top of his cardboard coffee cup. "She said, 'I would appreciate it enormously if you would stop calling me Mrs. Tyron. I am not a Mrs. I will never be a Mrs., and I have no fucking Fourth of July picnic to go to anyway.'"

And everyone laughed. Hilary's mother and father laughed and Bob laughed, even though, whenever they thought about this woman they grew frightened—her actions were so misguided when it came to life, when it came to men. But they laughed anyway and continued to laugh, hours later, when the doctor finally arrived to tell them what happened. Hilary would be fine, but there was a fetus that had fertilized outside her womb and had grown into her intestine and made her bleed two quarts of blood. The doctor said that Hilary's stomach was full of the stuff; she had lost so much blood that they were terrified the lack of potassium might make her heart stop.

"I just don't understand how she was walking around." The doctor smiled weakly, turned and walked down the hall.

"Hey, Doctor," Hilary's father called as he watched her disappear, "can you sew that thing up and keep her out of trouble?"

And they laughed again. They laughed out of relief.

When Bob sat in the waiting room with Hilary's parents and laughed, he thought he should probably call Nicholas and say, "Hey mate, you have bad aim," but he couldn't stand up. He could not get to the phone. He was thinking too much about her, feeling her only hours before. And he thought, yes, he did love her, he did! Now that he sat into the night, frightened that she might die, he felt the love was stronger and more sure. He climbed up the emergency exit stairs of the hospital and crawled into Hilary's bed beside her, careful of all the wires and tubes, and told her that yes, he did love her, he loved every part of her. He told her all of this even though he never really meant it. He told her this because she couldn't hear him now and would never know he ever said it. He wept quietly about the strangeness of it all as he pushed his face into the darkness of the cool crisp clinical sheets.

Hilary felt Bob's presence, not directly but indirectly in her dreams. She was fighting armies of men dressed in military regalia. She felt them trying to suffocate her, and this feeling was something she would never forget. When she awoke two days later, while her mother fed her chopped liver because her blood was all gone, she had this feeling inside, a certain knowing of having both survived and lost something important, but it was the loss that stayed with her. It burned and chortled.

A week later, Hilary walked out of the hospital very much alone. She carried a resolve, along with a note from Bob saying, "In San Francisco. Be back Saturday. Get Well Soon." She carried the note in one of her front pockets and climbed into a cab. As she drove away, she rolled down the window and looked back at the hospital. It was Boston Lying Inn Hospital, the same hospital where she was born, the only place she knew with a driveway shaped like a womb.

She imagined that many years down the road, she would be able to piece all the Bob stuff together. (She loved him; he didn't love her. He loved her; she didn't love him.) All the back and forth I do, I don't might make sense in time. They saw each other a few more times that summer, he always thoughtful of the stitches in her stomach. Still, she hoped they would talk some-day when they were all grown up and were able to see clearly. When they did talk ten years later, when they were both living in California, he in the north and she in the south, they were in their late thirties with lives of their own. He was happily married with two children, and she was still alone. They never spoke of it. In fact, they chatted about other things. Hilary talked about her paintings, her latest depression, and how her breasts were still giving her trouble. Even though she had them fixed, their nipples now pointing out, their real selves pointed in, mak-ing her look at the world and at the men who ran it in a funny, screwed-up way.

"You know how I love," she lied. "I am a whore for handsome men." And it was something in the way she said that word, was it whore or was it love, that made Bob laugh even though he was worried and a little sad. There were so many years, so much distance between them, but still he remembered Hilary so well. He remembered their time together, and just hearing her voice, he saw her twenty-year-old self turn to him a hundred times and imagined himself inside of her, and it made him hard again.

Hilary knew this. She sensed a shift in him by the sound of his laughter, the frightened pressing of silence and breath together, a symbol of sorts that told her that he had felt something too. It must have startled him. It startled her, but she was glad for it, even though for the life of her she could never give it a name.

We Americans

1

It began innocently enough. A man from El Salvador was tortured by fire. A man from Haiti fell from the sky in a big red weather balloon. A homeless woman in Santa Monica was run down by a Rolls. A twelve-year-old New Jersey boy died of leukemia. When Misha worked in television news, she became so overwhelmed with the sadness of the world that she wept in front of the cameras.

Exactly sixty-three days ago, thirty days after she lost her job for weeping, Misha began collecting tragedies like baseball cards.

She wrote the tragedies down, wrapped them in tiny Ziplock bags, and slipped the plastic packages into small jars of rose water, which she then placed on the mantelpiece under a painting of God. She surrounded her bottled tragedies with bouquets of wild sage she found on nearby mountaintops. She gave each bottle a name she had borrowed from the Bible: Peter for El Salvador; Paul for the man from Haiti; Mary for the woman run down; Matthew for the boy in New Jersey. On Saturdays, she burned the sage and cooked turkeys for the dead, malnourished, exploited, and unemployed.

For every sadness that Misha bottled, a red spot appeared on her skin. In places where it had been white and smooth, small explosions erupted in peculiar patterns. One morning she examined her body in a mirror and saw that her spots held shapes, as if foreign countries had imprinted themselves on her breasts, her belly, her wrists, her ankles, the inner parts of her thighs.

"My arm looks like Germany before the war," she told a doctor in the city. "And, look, there, down on my ankle, that is Vietnam, and here on the back of my neck, that is Nicaragua, and over here on my forehead, those bumps that you see are the Himalayas. And what about this on my wrist, it looks like Japan. But tell me, I'm concerned about the mountains. Are there mountains you know to be having trouble, political or otherwise?"

The doctor didn't think much of Misha and her suffering continents of skin, but Misha became convinced of something then: she was sadder beyond what she imagined sadness could be.

"Look at my tongue," she said, sticking it out. "Isn't that Bangladesh?"

"You have hives," the doctor said.

"But how do you know they are hives and not something else?"

"I'm a dermatologist."

Oh, she thought.

I collect tragedies in bottles and on my skin.

2

There was a night not too long ago. After the moon had gone away, Misha was left watching her television tragedies with a medium-size dog who wore an expression that always seemed to say this: I am perplexed by the state of the world and where I fit in it. I am a little nervous about it all, too.

That night, when Misha saw people's pictures on the news, her imagination flooded with their long faces and sad eyes. To make matters worse, she was homesick for snow, and it seemed to be snowing everywhere but where she was. It was snowing in New York, and in Moscow, and in places like that.

The news had been particularly stressful. A Hmong woman from Laos killed her five-year-old daughter and then jumped off a bridge onto the Hollywood Freeway. Misha bottled the woman and her daughter and placed them near the other recycled mustard and ketchup containers she had collected for Indochina. She reviewed her index cards on the issue but found only a question. The question was this:

If you kill one million people in five years, how many people are killed each hour, assuming the killers work a typical eight-hour day, Monday through Friday, with no time for lunch?

Misha named the woman Gloria and wrote down what she remembered from the news: the woman lived in North Hollywood with her husband, Wangy, and her daughter, Sara. They were very happy to be out of Laos. The Communists were still murdering the Hmong and others in Laos. That is why, the news said, no one for the life of them could understand why Gloria would kill herself, given she was living the good life in L.A. Cause of death Misha wrote at the bottom of the index card: *Gloria was sad. Her daughter was blind.*

The news said Gloria had taken her daughter to a sandbox in a nearby park. They showed pictures of the park so people like Misha could get a sense of what Gloria saw those few moments before she shot her little girl in the head with a .38. The camera lingered on the sandbox and shook slightly in the hands of the television cameraman who held it. Misha noticed it was a public sandbox and thought she saw a decapitated Ninja Turtle and splatters of the child's blood where the child must have fallen, as she imagined how Gloria must have sat there thinking about how she would do anything to spare this child the pain of being blind in the world.

Then the camera moved across the park, climbed the fence at its edge, and looked out over the freeway just like Gloria must have done earlier that evening, carrying her dead little girl over one shoulder. Misha focused on the steady flow of traffic below, the dripping headlights painting long flashing lines in the blackness, with road reflectors glittering here and there as she imagined Gloria jumping off the bridge with her daughter in her arms, falling into the middle of the freeway, the traffic moving a steady stream of light all the way from Hollywood to the ocean, the lights unrelenting and lonely, the car engines purring steady, careful to stay in their lanes. They stopped for nothing.

The dog groaned slightly as he rolled over, and Misha felt a large hot spot move into her belly. When she lifted her shirt, she saw a shape that resembled a leaning palm tree, a perfect island on her flesh that looked like Laos.

3

Misha never wins anything, so imagine her surprise at Thanksgiving when she received a notice from Vons supermarket in Pacific Palisades about this contest and how she had won twenty-five turkeys, these special baby Butter Ball turkeys that she could pick up anytime between such and such a date. So far she had been able to rationalize buying food at Vons versus some of the cheaper places because as she shopped she would eat handfuls of the chocolate-covered almonds they put out in bins, and this would even out all the money she had spent. And the turkeys helped with this reasoning. She would now think of Vons even more fondly and shop there even more often despite the fact that the guy who did the ads on the television—he owned the place—was so sweet and talked so often about the Vons family that it made her cringe. So you see, Misha had a lot of turkey in her downstairs freezer when the advertisement came on with the big-faced man talking about the Vons family. This is what happened. Right after the news about Gloria the television cut to rows and rows of delectable-looking vegetables and roast beefs and turkeys and the music swelled and suddenly everyone was singing while shopping at Vons.

Exactly sixty-three days before, Misha's husband left, telling her, "I feel like I could explode." This was how he put it. "I don't want to play with you anymore." He said this while he packed, throwing his things in a trunk. Throwing his possessions in her grandfather's steamer trunk that had wooden slats and stickers from Zermatt and Lake Como. Her husband said other things, too. "You're hard and judgmental." Then he threw a bunch of socks in his pack. "Your life vacillates between fear and anxiety about the state of the world." He threw in his shirts. "You can't relax. You can't have fun." He packed his pants. "You can't be happy." He laid in his blazers. "I won't take it anymore." He threw in some suits. "I won't do it anymore. I don't have to and I won't." He slammed everything in the trunk, dragged it out to his blue Acura Legend, and sped off. They were about to celebrate the tenth anniversary of making love for the first time. Since neither one of them could remember the exact date, Misha marked Pearl Harbor Day as the day. In retrospect, she believed this could have been a mistake.

4

Seventy-four hours before her husband left, President Bush gave his State of the Union address. This was an important speech because he had completely blown his trip to Japan.

The president had thrown up all over the Japanese.

But that night of the address, he said if he lowered this tax and that tax, Americans would have more money and could build more houses and people would buy more mortgages and developers could be rich and the banks would feel better because they could charge more interest and contractors and plumbers would work and those chubby guys—the ones with lovely wives and children with freckles who put the sprinkler systems in—would be very happy.

Misha began collecting tragedies in earnest when she heard this speech. The first bottle was the president. The second was her husband, John. She wrapped their faces in plastic and put them in jars. She then erected other monuments of sadness out of cardboard boxes for major battles and world wars and ethnic cleansings of the past. She began an inventory on index cards: natural disasters, the exploited, the unemployed, injustices, and wars in her lifetime. She explored libraries. She visited dermatologists. In the encyclopedia she found terms like paranoid, affective, anxiety, obsessive, compulsive, neurotic but could find nothing under S for sadness or skinless or C for compassion and complexities beyond reason. She made up her own name, *Compassion complexica nervosa*. She wrote it out on an index card. Below it she wrote: *People who suffer from compassion complexica nervosa are sad, have hives in shapes of foreign countries, have trouble watching the news.*

She searched for correlations between tragedies and times of the day, days of the week and holidays, noting that, like heart attacks, more injustices occurred on Monday mornings, wife abuse on Sundays, rapes on Saturdays, murders on Thursdays, and wars declared on Fridays. She also began tracking the days of the week world leaders were born on and was shocked to learn that Hitler, Mussolini, Richard Nixon, Henry Kissinger, and her husband were all born on the same day.

5

That night she saw Gloria Misha had Haiti on her ankle, New Jersey under her eye, Laos migrating across her chest and on her belly, and Los Angeles behind her ear. But Laos grew bigger, so she had a map of the country from her breasts to the base of her belly, with the Mekong River going down her leg. Her Laos burned and swelled, and in the center of her chest on a northern plateau known as the Plain of Jars Gloria's face appeared cradled in the valley of Misha's breasts. This apparition caused Misha to think about the woman's life. She wanted to ask her, *Gloria, what pushed you so far?* And when Misha did ask that and received no answer, she continued asking questions like, *Is it true that you lived in an upstairs apartment somewhere in Los Angeles where narrow streets bordered old-fashioned storefronts with green awnings? Did you live a real life versus a pretend one? Did you dream your dreams in color? Did you ride the bus? And is it true that you lived in a place with tan carpeting and light blue walls? And in the kitchen were there curtains with frills on the edges, and did you ever grow flowers on your porch out back?*

When Misha saw Gloria on the television, she had been alone in her house with her dog for one thousand, five hundred, and twelve hours. She had stopped brushing her teeth. She saw no one but the dermatologist, went nowhere but the library. The only real contact she had was her mother, who called from Florida once a week to tell her about drinking 100 proof vodka and swimming in the Gulf every day for half a mile. Her mother said that she missed Misha's dead father so much that every day just before she swam she would look up into the sky and plead for God to take her.

"I'm sorry, Mom," Misha said. "I miss him, too."

"Don't be silly," she said. "Say, did you read about the man who lost his arms in a machine? I saw an update today. *Arms Reattached. Farm Victim Goes Home.* Do you know what he said to the press? He said, 'I came to the hospital in three pieces and I'm going home in one.' This is a happy story. We need to think about happy things."

Before Misha's husband left, before he slammed that door for the last time, he told Misha that she reminded him of his mother, and just because he grew up with her oppressive nature then didn't mean he had to make the same choice now. This was how he put it. He was making a choice.

When Misha's husband left her, she felt like she wanted to die, too, and the only reason she couldn't was she was afraid her dog wouldn't have anyone to care for him. Misha loved her dog; she loved her dog like Gloria loved her child. His fat bottom reminded her of the turkey bottom when she put it in the oven, and when she put that turkey in the gas oven she patted the dog's bottom and told him, "You are one lucky dog that I don't bake you." She told the dog that particular thing at that moment in time because she remembered a story she had done about a man who tried to dry his poodle's hair in the microwave, and the dog exploded like a can of beans. This story was so sad that Misha cried when she reported it on the ten o'clock news, even though the man sued the microwave company and won. The man sued the company because the oven didn't have a warning that read, "Caution! Please don't put your dog in this oven, because he or she will explode!"

When Misha's husband walked out of the door for the last time, he told her that he had had it up to his ears and he felt like he could explode. That was his choice of words—up to his ears. "I feel like I could explode." When Misha basted the turkey, she dreamt about John's ears, and the way she used to suck on them, and felt sadness build inside her like tiny temblors.

But Misha reasoned that she was always sad around this time of year. She was sad because she felt sorry for all the turkeys that had to die. The news always showed the turkeys before they went to slaughter, and the same went for all the Christmas trees. She felt sorry for all the trees that had to die and then felt guilt because of all the Jews who were left out because everything centered on Christmas. And then she felt sad about the Holocaust and for people who threw themselves in front of cars on the freeway and thought about the Buddhist monk who burned himself up in the square in front of all those people in 1969 to protest the war. And then she looked at the other Asian people and felt bad about the bomb and didn't blame the Japanese for not wanting to say they were sorry about Pearl Harbor. She didn't blame them one bit.

6

That night Misha cooked the turkey she packed all her bottles and climbed into her car and drove down off the mountain where she had lived alone for one thousand, five hundred, and twelve hours without brushing her teeth. She drove through the town and got on the freeway. Besides her bottles she brought the dog, the turkey, bread, mayonnaise, and lemonade. She placed the turkey in a cooler because she had heard on the news about those awful diseases that breed in turkeys if they are left at room temperature.

When she arrived at the park where Gloria shot her daughter in the head with a .38, Misha sat on the edge of the sandbox with her dog and talked to Gloria. She had heard once about sudden and tragic deaths and how spirits stay around, so she suspected that Gloria would be there in one form or another. Misha closed her eyes and told Gloria how sorry she was about her life. "I am feeling bad about it all," Misha said, adding that she knew about what had happened in Laos. She knew about the CIA's secret Hmong army. She knew about Cambodia. She knew about Henry Kissinger and his three advisors, who, when they resigned, must have said, Henry, enough is enough, haven't we killed enough? And she imagined Henry, being only human, turning to them and saying, Look here, nobody has a monopoly on compassion.

7

The park was a great deal bigger than Misha had imagined and had many more trees than she thought possible for a city park in Burbank. At the far end was a long fence and below that the freeway. Misha sensed this was where Gloria must have jumped, but she was having trouble deciding exactly where. The dog and she walked silently in the dark up and down the freeway fence, and Misha was surprised at how many cars continued to drive in the middle of the night. Misha and the dog sat down every once in awhile to rest while Misha thought about what could have pushed Gloria so far. Misha had thought about suicide so often with great seriousness but never understood what exactly it could take to walk over that fine line of thinking versus doing.

The sun was rising slowly in gray tones, and behind it, on the other side of the world where Misha imagined Gloria must be, she saw vast gardens with large red flowers, and then she saw a man leaning over the fence looking at the freeway, and when she saw him, she realized this is where Gloria probably had jumped. But the man was what interested her then. Who was he? When did he get there? How did he come? He was carrying red flowers in his right hand while his left rested on the fence and his eyes looked down toward all the cars below. He threw the flowers on the freeway, turned away, and walked back to his car.

Pulling the dog, Misha followed the man through the park and then, once in her car, through the streets of North Hollywood until he stopped in front of a grocery market. She parked behind him. After a moment he climbed out of his car and threw back the wrought-iron gates to the market. The Sunday newspapers were stacked by the door. Misha rolled down her window.

"Good morning," she said.

The man nodded and smiled but offered nothing else as he began carrying the papers inside. Misha climbed out of her car and watched him as she thought about how she would expect him to close for the day, just stop everything. But he didn't. He carried newspapers and pasted up all the new signs for the specials and told Misha about how the economy was sluggish. "We sell sixty turkeys every year," he said. "Every year it is the same, no more, no less. This year we sold only twenty-five."

He shook his head. "The economy is slow, it is very very bad."

Misha told him she had seen the news and was sorry. His face went blank and she thought maybe she had the wrong place. She couldn't tell. In fact, she didn't know if he was Vietnamese or Korean or Chinese or Thai, but by then it didn't matter. She opened the back of the car and told him that she had brought him a turkey. She had cooked it especially for him. He seemed confused, she could see it in his face, but he looked at the turkey and back at her and nodded his head. "Turkey?" he asked.

She nodded and he waved her inside. She picked up the cooler and followed him through the aisle filled with mops and sponges. Once at the back of the store, he opened a door that led to a room where they sat on boxes amidst other boxes of dog food, Tampax, and cranberry juice.

"Do you like mayonnaise and white bread?" she asked. "Because this is the best way to eat cold turkey. In a sandwich."

"Sure," he said, but later when Misha saw him study all four corners of his sandwich as if he were examining a strange insect, she knew he was just being agreeable. He told her about the economy again. "Everybody is writing bad checks." He also talked about how in the grocery business he got to meet all kinds. Misha smiled at him. He was a fine man and he had a nice store with long aisles and a fair selection of wine. She told him about Vons and how she had won so many turkeys she didn't know what to do or how to feel about it.

"Ah, America." The man shook his head. "I am up to my ears in turkey."

They laughed about that and when it grew silent again, Misha felt her chest and belly burn with Laos.

"Yeah," she said flatly. "Up to our ears in turkey with Laos under our skin."

"Laos," he said, smiling. "You know Laos?"

"I am Laos," she said and she lifted her shirt for him to see.

Whose World Is This?

That night, the night before William left me for good, I lay awake and asked myself what would happen if I closed off all my senses except for sight. If I plugged my ears, my nose, cut out my tongue, taped my fingers, just shut the door to all my senses, could my eyes possibly compensate for my loss? Could I see more? Could I see myself for who I was? Could I possibly know from here what I might find there? Then?

There is only freedom in not wanting. This is what William had told me. And my problem was wanting. My problem was desire. Hannah, you always want this or that, he said. You have to understand that this is not the true nature of things. This wanting business makes you small. It makes your mind go to places it shouldn't go. Life only opens if you accept. Now.

Sometimes during those afternoons the California sunlight flew through the windows like tiny golden volleyballs and William laughed and chased me all around the house. *There are some things that you just come to know,* he teased. *With patience, baby, there are some things you just come to know* and with a *whoosh* and a *bang* we flew down the hall, me running, William close behind, his wheelchair buzzing like a fly, its wheels squeaking and grinding against the shiny wooden planks. He was fast and the air felt heavy like rain. It occurred to me one afternoon as I fell to the floor that I didn't want to run anymore. I played possum instead. Played dead. Played still. I watched him upside down and, holding my breath, he grew crooked and strange like in a dream, the sunlight moving around him, faster than speeding bullets, faster than the speed of sound. The motor stalled, and William flipped his elbow several times to hit the control forward, but it was a random motion, luck of the draw; sometimes he couldn't move at all.

"Transmitting," he said, staring at his fingers.

I pushed myself up and slipped my arms around him. "Transmitting," I repeated, tightening my hold and feeling him then, cold and awkward. I felt sad, and because he was paralyzed, I felt I had the right to this sadness.

I met William in the spring of 1976, when I was working the graveyard shift at a nursing home in a town called Locke, a nowhere town east of San Francisco where the Sacramento River wound around levees and dams and the bars that lined Main Street had flashing neon martini glasses out front. I was twenty-six or -seven and doing a lot of drugs, trying to find God, trying to figure out how many men I could make love me at the same time. I think there were four of them before William, all boys I met at a bar in town named the Bighorn, all boys who couldn't get their eyes to meet mine straight on, and this was the first thing I noticed about William: he looked me in the eyes and when he did, the others drifted away, one by one.

Graveyard meant I worked from midnight to seven in shifts of three. Each shift I turned twenty bodies to ensure each body would stay in one place for only so long. It didn't matter, because people's bodies had minds of their own. Deep sores dug into bony hips like small gaping mouths, and sometimes late at night when I looked into these mouths I saw these wounds churn into rosy throats and at the bottom where I imagined voices would call, a wall of bone, white and stony glaring out at me. Tending to these people was always harder, taking more time to roll bodies and change bandages, taking more drugs to get through. I was working that shift the night I first met William. I had just finished my first round when I walked into the empty room at the end of the hall. The room had been empty for months, and I went in there sometimes to turn my back on the night, to summon peace, but invariably as I lay there I replayed my nights over in my head. *Mrs. Harper wasn't eating. May had seemed angrier than usual. Mr. Schultz was on his way out.* And I would always be left with imagining that moment when I watched the light leave these people's eyes. In an instant, whatever there was would be gone and I found myself afraid I would die, too. I had dreams of talking to dead men in caskets, dreams where I saw phantoms wearing purple knee bands jumping out at me to slit my throat, but that night when I first opened the door to this room, I forgot all this because there was this handsome man, my age, maybe a little older, lying flat, not out of choice but out of necessity.

"Oh my God." I jumped back. "You scared me."

"Am I that frightening?" he asked.

"No, you just—" I said. "I didn't know you were here."

Each room had small fluorescent tubes of light sandwiched into the seams where the ceiling met the walls. It was a strange otherworldly kind of light, dim and shadowy. I stood in the doorway a moment and within a second I heard the motor of the bed, and his head and upper body rose as the back of the bed moved him forward almost to a sitting position. He had the switch in his mouth, operating the button with his tongue. He spit out the switch and watched it drop as if checking its progress and then looked up at me and smiled.

"I thought everybody had gone home," he said, "and I was bumming because I am really hungry."

"No, there's a graveyard shift."

"I knew that," he said, "but it has been hours since I have seen a soul. Is there anything to eat?"

"No," I said, "not really. There's a machine with peanuts."

"Would you do me a favor, then? There's money in the drawer. Could you, I mean *would you*, get me a doughnut, a real honey-dipped doughnut, make that two, at Mister Doughnut, and a raspberry jelly, with regular coffee, a large, extra cream, and double sugar? I can't stand the shit they serve here, and I'm starving to death."

His hair was long, I could tell that, and his eyes were light, a mix of blue and green. He wore a turquoise T-shirt, which seemed normal enough, but his body—his arms, his legs, his feet—lay still in separate ways as if they were strangers headed down different roads and I thought, *This is a crime. This is a fucking crime.*

He placed his head back and closed his eyes, as if he were exhausted by the speed or the lightheartedness of his words. I couldn't tell which. I was too stunned. I had never imagined a paralyzed man could be so handsome or sound so happy.

I walked into the room and leaned on the steel rails at the end of the bed.

"I'm Hannah," I said.

After a moment he opened his eyes and I watched the ocean color fade and drift around his face like smoke.

"William," he smiled.

"When did you get here?" I asked.

"Yesterday, I think."

"But why here?"

"In between, I guess. I've just spent about six months in the hospital." He looked around the room. "And now . . . Well, I guess this is where they put people like me. Apparently."

"Oh," I said, pulling my hair away from my face.

"I'm trying to get back to school," he said.

I walked around the bed, checked the catheter bag, and then stood there looking at him, not knowing what to say.

"It's late," I said. "It's like two."

"I know."

"Do you need something to sleep? I can call the nurse to get you—"

"No."

"Do you need anything?" I asked. "Do you need to be moved? Do you need a drink?"

He looked around the room and back at me, confused by my concern.

"I think everything is in order, but as I said, doughnuts would be cool."

"Okay, I'll get your doughnuts," I said. "But you'll have to wait until I'm on break."

"How long is that? I am starving."

I looked around. I didn't have a watch. "Soon, man. I'll do it as soon as I can."

Four girls were all we had on the graveyard shift. Some of us worked swing. I preferred graveyard. The patients were asleep, and taking care of them was easier in darkness. The urine smell was down at night. The old people didn't pee as much, or maybe it had something to do with how the sunlight affected things. Anyway, everything seemed happier, more manageable at night. We had breaks, fifteen minutes or so at a time, and then in the funny yellow light of the coffee room we'd snort drugs, smoke cigarettes, talk about our boyfriends and all the old people in the home. We had grown fond of the old people over time. It was hard to see them live and die in these sterile rooms with nobody there. All that and the fact that the place smelled of urine, but this was the odd thing. The smell kind of grew on you, became part of you. This is what the girls said on their breaks in the hot lights of the coffee room. *This kind of thing becomes part of you.* But we usually had only fifteen minutes to talk about it and then we got up, high as hell, to go roll the people. The beds were set up so one could roll the person and the sheets at the same time. It was a trick with the sheets. That's what I remember. Tricks with sheets, long halls of darkness, and all the doors. At three in the morning it was an endless hell of doors and drugs and rolling souls like piles of manure.

I had no business being there. I had no business being any-where, because I was a drug addict. Black beauties mostly, when I could get them, and if not, coke and white cross, little white pills with plus signs, which I liked to swallow three at a time. If I couldn't get those, anything at all.

There weren't very many nurses on at night. Josy was one, an LVN and drug dealer, mostly coke, some speed. She worked the same shifts I did, so throughout that winter and spring at the nursing home we managed to have some fun. The problem with Josy was that she cut her fast drugs, but I could forgive her for that. She needed the money. She had a three-year-old daughter at home and a boyfriend named Cam who came in and out of her life, making her crazy.

Most nights after I checked in on my wing and Josy had done her meds we'd meet up, have coffee, snort drugs, and talk about Cam. He was a mean man, tall and big-boned who beat the hell out of her whenever he felt like it, but each night when she'd go on about him, *how sweet he was, what a doll he was,* all I could think about were the bruises and black eyes and I felt rage swallow me. I wanted to stand up and scream, *What the hell gives him the right, the motherfucker.* But I couldn't stand, because I was too high and too ashamed, seeing myself and my skinny girlfriend, drugged and dead, dressed in white polyester and tennis shoes, walking dark halls with our bloodshot eyes and stringy long hair sucked moist in clumps, caught between our teeth from all the chewing.

Spring nights in Locke were cool and calm and I felt hopeful sometimes when I visited an old woman named May. She was about ninety, a retired telephone operator from Sacramento who reminded me of my own grandmother, her old blue eyes and thinly skinned hands holding mine. May always asked the same question over and over. *Dear, how are things? How are things in your world?* We often went outside together to watch the night sky. May was an expert in stars and flowers so she liked to talk on about both. When she felt strong, she walked with her walker, surveying the gardens in the courtyard. *Look how sad the coleus is, Hannah. Doesn't anybody water?*

Sometimes she'd sing to the plants or tell a story, stopping and teetering a bit and then reaching for my hand. *Oh Hannah, your hands are so tiny! My mother had tiny hands, too.*

When she was tired, I'd take her out in her wheelchair and stand behind her. I loved to watch her, because when she moved her face toward the sky, her white hair drooped behind her neck like clouds and she'd talk nonstop about nothing at all. *I don't know how it is in your world, but in my world . . . Ring-a-ling. Burt, is that you? Don't talk to me about heaven. What the hell do you know about heaven.*

After I left William, I went to check in on May, and from the doorway leading to her room I could see the white cloth ties cinched around her waist and her hands tied to the arms of the chair, and I knew something was terribly wrong. She was asleep so I walked quietly into the room and bent down in front of her, placing a hand on her shoulder. "May," I said quietly. "May, it's Hannah." She didn't move so I reached around the back of the chair to untie the restraints. "May," I said again, placing my hand on her forehead, and within a second her eyes snapped open and she started to scream, flailing her arms to push me away, hitting me so hard in the face that my nose started bleeding again. I must have yelled, because Josy came running in, finding me holding my nose with one hand while trying to hold May down with the other.

"Your nose. You ass," she said as she took over May. "Your nose is bleeding again."

"I know," I said.

"Well, hold your head back."

I stood there while Josy retied the restraints. May was scream-ing, "Don't touch me," and I started crying because I felt so bad for May and because I couldn't feel my nose anymore. It didn't feel like a nose. It felt separate.

"You can't be doing that for her anymore," Josy said as she led me into the bathroom. "She's out of her mind."

Josy turned back and took my hand. "Now let's get a look at you."

She led me to the sinks and gently took my hand away from my nose, and the blood came gushing out. "You better lie down."

There was blood all over my white uniform and I was still crying.

"Josy, I think I have a hole in it."

The blood kept pouring out and she stuck her slim fingers up my bloody nose and felt around.

"I can't feel my nose, and then I can, and when I do, man, it hurts."

"Yeah, girl. You got a hole in it, you better use the other side."

She looked at me with her translucent green eyes and I began to laugh, sending blood around the room in sprays.

"Shhh," she said. "Shut up, you fool. You're getting blood everywhere."

But I couldn't stop. It was that weird release, a sobbing disguised as laughter.

"Oh man, you are really fucked up. You're not snorting that speed, too." And as if she answered the question herself, she reached into her pocket and held up a yellow downer of some kind.

"Eat this." She put it in my mouth.

"What is it?" I asked.

"Chew," she said. "One two three, chew."

She moved toward the back of the bathroom, got out her keys, and opened the closet. I was beginning to feel cold on the floor, holding my nose on.

"I think there's a uniform in here that might fit you," she said. "You're all bloody."

I tipped my head forward and saw my chest covered in blood.

"I'm hemorrhaging, Josy. I could be dying right now."

I lay back down and began crying again.

"What?" she asked, her voice muffled from inside the closet.

"All of it," I said. "May, you, me. All the blood here."

Josy walked back, holding out a uniform.

"Girl, you need to get your *stuff* together. Big time together. You are falling apart. Doing too much of that bad stuff. Get up." She pushed me with her foot. "Slow, now, and hold it tight."

I sat up and the blood started again.

"Shit," she said. "Get down. Stop crying. It's not helping anything."

I lay down and felt the cool tiles on my back. I heard the water running and felt Josy place some cold paper towels on my nose. I looked at Josy then. She was my friend. Her skin was the color of nutmeg, but she had these green eyes—the most amazing color I had ever seen.

"Josy, hasn't anyone ever told that you have the most a m a z i n g—"

And then the intercom sounded, asking for a nurse in room 40A. "It's May," Josy said. "Hold on to these. It will stop."

I lay there a long time before the bleeding finally stopped, and as I did I felt absolutely drenched in sadness. I wanted to run to Josy and tell her about May. *She's not crazy, she's just old,* but I couldn't move. I touched my legs and then moved my hands up my stomach, running them over my breasts and around my face, and when I felt my heart still doing somersaults, I pretended I couldn't feel it. I pretended I couldn't move. I played possum. Played dead and I smiled a little about that because it made me think of the stories I had heard about possums. I lay there a little while longer thinking about how terrific it would feel to be a possum with its weird little eyes and little pink skin.

Later that night, when the downer had kicked in and I was able to scrape myself up off the floor and into another uniform, I went around the corner to get William doughnuts. There was no way I could drive and it wasn't like it was very far. A few blocks, maybe, I don't know, it seemed like forever. Time stopped, which was good, because when I got to William's room, my heart felt warm and calm, pleasant and numb over the grinding mess of cocaine.

He was asleep, so I sat in the dark for a while and watched him. I was only there for a few minutes before I grew to wonder what it felt like, or, rather, what it didn't feel like, when one could not roll over in one's sleep. He looked uncomfortable, so I got up and tried to move his legs.

"I'm not asleep," he said. "Can't you see my eyes are open?"

"No."

"I've been watching you. What are you doing?"

"You looked uncomfortable. I was trying to . . . Well, I got your doughnuts."

I stood there for a moment when it occurred to me I had to feed him, and it felt strange. I had done many things with men. I had done them with skill and ingenuity. I had done them with my hands, my mouth, and my tongue, but I had never fed a man, young like William. I didn't know where to begin. I put my hands on my hips and watched him, praying he wouldn't see that I was frozen in place, when I noticed his fingers were moving, not shaking, but actually moving with purpose like he was playing an imaginary musical instrument. Finally, I turned on the bedside light.

"Your fingers are moving," I said.

"I know. They do that."

"How come? If the nerves are severed, how can your fingers move?"

"Not severed, just damaged. Anyway, you know the thing about fingers, they have minds of their own."

"Right," I huffed in disbelief. "I'll remember that. Do you want your doughnuts?"

"Yes, but I can't eat lying down. The switch fell."

I hunted around for it, reaching over him, following the cord's trail from his shoulder. When I pressed the switch, he came up slumping to the side. I placed my hands on his shoulders and pulled him straight. He felt light, a bag of crooked bones.

"What do you want first?" I asked, sitting on the side of the bed. "Doughnut or coffee?"

"Coffee. Then I want the honey doughnut dipped in the coffee."

I put the cup up to his mouth and he sipped. I tore off a piece of the doughnut and soaked it in the coffee and then placed the dripping doughnut into his open mouth. He chewed, smiling, making noises of pleasure. This is how we spent the next fifteen minutes or so, talking little.

When he had eaten everything, I finally asked what had happened, how he had become paralyzed. He didn't seem at all shocked at the question.

"A car accident."

I must have grimaced, because he looked like he wanted to reach out and touch me.

"I didn't feel a thing, but in that split second when the car began to spin, I knew everything there was to know."

He smiled and it was then I noticed the absence of something. It took only a moment to realize what was missing. It was the simple gesture of a shrug. That's what should have happened. He should have shrugged, but he didn't. He just looked at me wearing this shit-eating grin.

Pine Manor had about forty rooms, ten per wing, and together all four wings A, B, C, D came around into a perfect square. William lived in the last room on D, so for the next few weeks I made sure I was assigned to the D wing. I was curious about him. I had never known anyone who was paralyzed. I had seen them, I had felt sorry for them, but I had never known them. So almost every night I went to William's room and sat at the end of his bed in the dark. Sometimes I watched him sleep. Other times, when he was awake, we'd talk. He was a funny man, half prophet, half crazy person who told me he could read minds, past, and future. I never believed him, of course, but I liked him immediately. Unlike others I knew, he seemed to prefer talking about life in very abstract ways. One of his favorite things was to talk about people as if they were fruit or vegetables. He thought of himself as a root vegetable, like a yam or a rutabaga. Josy was an asparagus, May a tomato, but he told me I couldn't be a vegetable.

"You have a fruit aura," he said. "An exotic fruit like a pomegranate or a pineapple, something you need to crack open to find the goodies."

"What do you mean by that?"

"Not that you're not beautiful, you are," he said. "But your real beauty is hiding."

"Behind what?"

"Why don't you tell me?"

"What are you talking about?" I asked.

"You're a speed freak," he said. "I can tell a mile away."

"You don't know anything."

"I know a drug freak when I see one."

"What does that say about you?" I asked.

"I know the road, I guess," he smiled. "It tells you I know the road." He hesitated a moment and looked the other way.

"Maybe we should get the old lady and go for a stroll."

William was another night traveler, so he liked to come with me when I took May out. Once I managed to get him into his chair he followed me down the halls into May's room and then outside. Nothing important happened in the courtyard. In fact, we talked very little, most nights just watching the sky. William and May lined up in their wheelchairs with me on the cement bench behind them. May sometimes would go on about something, about the sky, about the world, and when she talked, we half listened. Otherwise we just sat, William studying the sky as if it had answers, and me studying William in the same way.

William's room got morning sun, and it wasn't long before I made it a habit to say good-bye before I went home. I opened the curtains, washed his face with a warm washcloth. He often moaned and asked me to hold his hands and then asked me to rub him with lotion, maybe coconut or cocoa butter or something else he could smell. He didn't say so, but I thought he was trying to feel again.

When I rubbed him, his back, and his chest, he sometimes told me I was beautiful.

"Perfect beauty," he said. "I like that."

William sang in his sleep. He sang songs from *Hello Dolly, My Fair Lady, The Music Man, Oklahoma,* and at night sometimes I sat outside his room and listened. One night he sang almost all the songs from *Hair.*

"Was that you last night?" I asked.

He looked at me blankly from the bed.

"Last night singing. I thought I heard you singing *Hair.*"

I walked across the room and opened the blinds. The windows overlooked the courtyard. It was early.

"Hell no. Don't know any songs from *Hair,* don't know how to sing either."

He was smiling.

"What kind of person is that, a person who can't sing?" I asked.

"The same kind of person who can't walk, I suppose."

"Maybe you sing in your sleep?"

"Nah. I'm a sleepwalker."

"Unlikely," I said.

"Unlikely, but not impossible."

"Sure," I said. "Can you whistle?"

"Nah."

"Give it a try. Whistle."

He puckered his lips and whistled the first few bars of "Everything's Up-to-Date in Kansas City."

"Ah, good lord, *you*."

"*You*," he repeated. "Great song. They've gone about as fur as they c'n go!"

I stood at the end of his bed.

"I have a helluva sense of humor," he said.

"Noticed that," I said.

"On your way home?"

"Yeah," I said.

"Still doing speed?"

"No," I lied.

"If I could look, what would I find in your pocket?"

"What do you know? You don't know anything."

"Four reds. Two blues. Fifteen plus."

I turned my pockets inside out to show him they were empty. The truth was, I stashed my drugs in my bra and anyway, Josy was out of fast drugs, and I was doing downers I stole from her drug cart: Haldol, Valium, Miltown, and Demerol. The high was good doing those things. I grew to like the feeling of going down.

"Will you?" He made a quick motion with his head.

"But we've tried it," I said.

"More," he said. "Please."

I walked over to him, releasing the bed rail and pulling back the sheets. He was beautiful even if he couldn't move.

"Almond or peppermint?" I asked.

"Cocoa," he said.

I reached into the bedside table's cabinet and pulled out a bottle of cocoa butter lotion. I poured it into my hands, rubbing them together to make them warm, and placed my hands on his chest, silent. I began to move them around up to his shoulders and down onto his stomach, rubbing. He felt cold.

"Lower," he said.

"William."

"Give a dead man a hand job," he said, closing his eyes. "Say yes."

"X marks the spot," I said as I marked a big X on his chest. "Do you remember that game? With a dot, dot, dot and a dash, dash, dash and a big question mark."

I moved my hands willy-nilly up and down his body.

"Shivers going up. Shivers going down. Shivers going all around? Do you feel this?" I asked.

He nodded. I cupped one hand palm down onto the top of his head and then slapped it with my other hand, making a soft cracking sound.

"A crack of an egg," I said and stopped. "I forgot the rest."

I tried it again. "A crack of an egg . . ." I pulled my hands away. "I'm tired," I said. "I've been here all night."

I smiled at him. I liked these feelings of exhaustion, as if the drugs pushed it farther. I felt pleasantly numb most of the time.

"My face? You won't do my face?"

I poured more lotion on my hands and gently rubbed his face, up around his forehead, his eyes, his nose, around the back of his ears, then down his neck, then around his mouth. He pushed out his tongue and licked my hand.

"As long as I have a face, babe . . ."

I took my hands away and glared at him. He laughed.

"Could be good." He smiled, lifting his eyebrows.

"You make it impossible to be nice to you."

"Come on—it's easy to be nice to a cripple," he said. "Isn't that the thing with the uniform?" He stopped. "It was a miracle," he said with a sudden serious tone. "When all of a sudden he could feel her touch."

"Fuck you," I said.

"Never," he laughed. I reached down and kissed him hard on the mouth, and he slipped me the most incredible tongue.

"Fuck you," I said again.

"You'd die trying," he said. "You'd die."

I lived upriver from the nursing home across a steel drawbridge in a small blue cabin with a fig tree out my window in an old motel motor court with other blue cabins with white shutters. In those days, the place, maybe ten cabins in all, was run by a woman named Lydia. She was about sixty with dyed black hair and she had a body shaped like a potato with legs. When I told William this, he laughed.

I liked Lydia, I told him. She had spirit. She drank her vodka from the bottle straight up and yelled things like "Let them, let them eat figs for Christ's sakes!" at the top of her lungs, any time of the day, for no reason at all. She reminded me of my mother in her inappropriateness, in her crassness, and I will always remember her because of that, and the figs, and because she had a boyfriend named Richard whom she called Dick. When I met up with them taking out the trash or hanging around the pool, she always said, "Have you met my Dick? My Dick," and she laughed, her body shaking, her plastic yellowed teeth shining in the air.

"William, you know the first time I met Lydia she looked at me and said this, 'Jesus, sister, you have a set of the biggest tits I have ever seen. Heavens mercy almighty. Dick, take a look. It's fucking tragic.'

"You hardly ever meet women like that anymore," I said. "Women who say things like that. Women who tell it like it is."

"Let me see them," he said.

I looked at him a moment in disbelief.

"Let me see them. They don't look so tragic to me."

And as I pulled up my shirt for him to see, he told me they were grand, but every part of me was grand, and Lydia was just mean. I was perplexed because I had thought many things about Lydia but I never thought she was mean and then he asked me to kiss him and when I did, I remembered the feeling I knew when in love and doing drugs. It was a matter of shifting, like flying perhaps, but more like a twisting into a new world, a world within reason, a world of hope and faith with gods and things. It was as simple as that. The colored pills and powders were just symbols, popping and snorting rituals. Red for promise. Black for desire. White for love and like that. But that summer, after I met William, things began to change. It wasn't coherent or deliberate, it just happened like spells of bad weather happen, and a part of me knew, like addicts know, I was going down. The question was, How far could I go and how long would it take to get there.

William told me to think of it like this. Imagine you're on a train. You know where you're headed. You can get off or follow it to the end.

By then we had learned to make love, but it was a random love, like William's moves, luck of the draw. On the days he came home with me I would strip him of all his clothes and me of mine and we'd lie in bed facing each other in darkness, William propped on his side with a bank of pillows, and he would tell me how it would feel if it could happen. Each moment. Blow by blow. And when he went on like this so assured, it was stunning how he could ease me into feeling with his words. And there were times when I could get high enough, I would make grand stands and, taking part of his penis in my mouth, say let's give it a whirl, and when it didn't work, I cried and told him I loved him and he said it was not love that I was feeling. It was pity. "All the sadness you feel for me is really your own."

In late June William came to stay with me before heading off to school. Lydia and Dick set up the cabin so he could get around. There were only three rooms, but they were large and I didn't have very much furniture, so he could wheel around from room to room. While I was at work, Lydia and Dick spent time with him or when they weren't with him he read Gurdjieff and other mystics, Sufis, and Zen, turning the pages of his worn books with his teeth on this special contraption designed for quadriplegics. I fed him, I bathed him, I became expert at moving his body around from chair to couch to bed to chair to couch to bed, always pleasantly numb and buzzing from the painkillers and Seconals I stole from the nursing home and the speed that I could occasionally get from Josy.

In the mornings when I came home I watched him sleep before I woke him and fed him breakfast. I sat in a chair next to my bed, sentimental and sad from the drugs the night before, always wishing when he woke up he could reach out to hold me.

"Hannah, I am okay like this," he said one morning. "Really. Come here."

I climbed into bed and as I lay with him, careful to keep my eyes open, I listened to the sounds of his breathing and thought about the songs he hummed in his sleep and all that he had told me. Love is an act of faith, he had said, and during those days I groped for this kind of understanding in darkness. I dreamt of knowing this deeply as I dreamt of knowing the things he knew, as if he had answers I could know by keeping my eyes wide open while wrapping my body around his deadened one in sleep. If I was able to find the right combination of drugs, I could sleep, but I never looked forward to this, because my dreams were always the same. I was blind and cold lying somewhere always feeling little fingers struggling to open my eyes. William said it wasn't forever. Whatever it was, it wasn't forever. And he stayed beside me during these times and watched me sweat and shake with odd fevers and strange nightlike visitors poking at my eyes.

By August I had found another job in Sacramento, so I was working at the nursing home only a few nights a week. I would still visit May whenever I could, but during the days I worked counseling fat people on how not to be fat. The place was called The Stress and Habit Control Center and was run by a reformed Scientologist who had become a sociologist and hypnotist, a guy named Dr. Roger Bayne, who paid me two hundred dollars a week, plus a bag of dope, Humboldt dope, no big thing. He hypnotized me a few times so I would know what it was about. The last time he sat me down in a small white room in a brown vinyl reclining chair, asked me to close my eyes, and then talked me down a long set of stone steps in my head. At the bottom was a river and a boat waiting for me. I got in the boat and he guided me down this river to a dock, where he asked me to get out and then look at my feet.

"What do you see?" he asked.

"I don't know," I said.

"What are you wearing on your feet?"

"I have no feet."

"You must have feet. Everyone has feet. Feel your legs."

"I have no legs."

"Look up," he said. "What do you see?"

"I see an old woman's head doing somersaults."

"Ask her a question."

"Who are you?" I asked.

"What does she say?" he asked.

"Who wants to know? Her face is bleeding and she's asking who wants to know?"

When I opened my eyes, Dr. Bayne wore an expression that seemed to say, *I am worried about you,* but he kept me on anyway, paying me to dress up like I knew something about people and sit in a room full of mirrors and make these people who wanted to be thin eat their favorite foods. The people, some weren't so fat, walked in carrying bags of potato chips and Cheetos and Big Macs and things and there we sat while they chewed it all up and spit it out into a pink napkin so I could tell them stories about where the food went and how it really did not have their best interests at heart.

"This food here hates you," I said. "It really does. It's trying to trip you up." And I held up a big jar full of fat in formaldehyde for them to see—it took two hands to hold—and their reaction, no matter who they were, was always the same. Their mouths would drop as their eyes dulled a notch with a distancing waver. *I am shutting off now,* they signaled. *I am shutting o-f-f.*

It was another irony, another lie I lived. I had no business being there telling these people these things, and one afternoon I met a woman who told me just that. She had brought a perfectly beautiful apricot pie that she had made from scratch. I looked at her, the delicious folds in her old skin, her bright brown eyes, and thought, *Hannah, you will never be a woman like this.*

She told me she had picked the apricots from a tree in her yard and she loved these apricots so dearly she waited every year for them to come ripe, and every year she gained five lousy pounds, and over the years that added up. *But you're beautiful,* I wanted to say. *But this pie is beautiful.*

I looked at her hands and thought, *These are the hands of a woman who loved apricots.* The skin was luminous, nurtured, and thin. I could see her purple veins and the peach color on her nails move in waves as her fingers kneaded the straps of her black leather bag. I looked at my own hands, empty and sad, and felt frightened because I didn't know what I loved anymore.

"These apricots here hate you," I said. Her face snapped in stillness, her smile and eyes flickered gently as if she was saying, *Please be kind to me, I am only trying to understand this love of apricots.*

"They hate you," I repeated. She winced in disbelief and I found myself trying to imagine what it felt like to be a woman happy picking something as stupid as apricots and placing them lovingly one by one in a basket. I began to cry. William was leaving the following morning and I realized I had gone as low as I could go with this woman and in spite of all of it she leaned over and took my hand and squeezed it. "This must be very hard on you," she said. "This must be very hard."

When I got home that evening, I found William packed and ready to go and celebrating with Dick and Lydia by the pool.

"Hannah," Lydia howled when she heard my car door slam. I walked toward them across the front lawn. They huddled together around a table under a dirty gray umbrella. Lydia was drunk; I could see that from the dreamy expression that comes from too much alcohol, and for the first time it made me feel afraid.

"Hey baby," William said. He dropped his head down and sipped something from a long red-and-white-striped straw that poked out of his glass. Directly behind them was a cliff that led up to a mesa. The sky hung over it with streaks of red, and I thought briefly again about that woman and her apricots. She had been so kind.

I sat down next to them.

William looked at me, rolling his eyes. "I lost my socks," he said.

"He moved his foot," Lydia said. "Getting ready for his trip."

Dick pushed a basket full of chips at me.

"Eat something, darlin'," he said. "You look like you need something to eat."

He smiled and his aftershave drifted at me in waves. I turned away and looked at William.

"You shouldn't be drinking," I said. "You know how sick it makes you."

"Look who's talking," Lydia chortled. "Our resident druggie."

Dick turned to her. "Lydia, you're being belligerent to our friend here. Our little Hannah who looks so sad today."

"What's new," she snorted. "Ms. Pathetic."

She got up and teetered toward her cabin to get herself another drink.

"I just don't want to be the one who has to dig the shit out of you," I said to William. "I'm tired of digging shit out of you."

"Nobody has asked you to dig the shit out of me," he said. "It's been your choice all along."

In the middle of the bathroom, in the middle of the floor, under the fifth plank is a silver box of my mother's where I hide my drugs. When I found myself there later, after I had put William to bed, I saw that they were gone.

"Tell me where you put my drugs," I asked him. "Tell me."

I rolled him over to face me and stood there as long as I could before finally leaving the room, walking around the house, turning on all the lights, and pulling open all his boxes, suitcases, drawers, the closets, more drawers, hunting frantically in pockets, in corners, under rugs, searching for help and hope in small packages that I could swallow.

"William," I screamed, "tell me where they are."

He opened his eyes but said nothing.

"Tell me," I said.

He turned away. "No."

I don't remember all the details of pulling him from the bed and dragging him into the living room, but I do remember begging, and I do remember seeing him alone on the floor, struggling, his eyes stunned and blinking as his mouth kept saying "No."

"Move," I said. "If you can do that, you can move. I want you to move, damn it."

He only looked at me and blinked. As I watched him, I listened to the knocks and whirls of the night, and when everything grew still, I closed my eyes and saw myself in him, in different pieces thrown all over the floor. *If a woman has no strength or courage,* I asked myself, *what then?*

I walked in circles and thought about how odd it felt to be so out of control. To actually feel so terrified and so enraged.

Then I saw him move. I saw the son of a bitch move.

"Hannah," he said, his legs moving phantom moves. He looked like he was running in place.

"Hannah," he repeated like he was asking a question, and I couldn't see him anymore.

I left him there and walked outside. I walked around the house, holding my eyes open with my fingers, and looked inside through all the windows. This was a great comfort to me, looking inside on a life as if it belonged to somebody else, and through these windows I watched William on the floor. His legs were still, his body lay in a chaotic lump. I watched him from all different windows and thought about how much I hated myself for doing this to him, how much I hated myself, indeed.

"Hannah," he called. I couldn't hear him, but I saw his mouth move. I knocked on the window. He turned toward me. "Come back," he said.

I stretched the palms of my hands against the window. I wanted to scream, "Help me," but all I could say was "I can't."

I turned away and walked up around the back of the house on a trail that led to the mesa. I walked for hours and later, when I got home and found William asleep on the floor, I straightened his legs and his arms and covered him with a blanket. After a moment of watching him, I climbed on top of him, touching his nose, his lips, and the tops of his eyes with my fingers.

"Will you please stay with me a little longer?" I asked.

He laughed. "Why in the world would I stay with someone who would throw me out of bed for drugs? Really, Hannah, you're too tortured for words."

"I'll die if you go."

"No you won't. You're too stubborn."

"Please?"

"It's time for me to go."

I got up again and turned off all the lights and lay down next to him. It was dark so it took a minute for my eyes to adjust, but soon the smooth buttery light from the moon and the stars illuminated his still figure, lying on his back, his hands on his stomach and below that the bump of his penis and catheter. I shimmied myself down his body so I could easily see both him and the sky through the window and lay like that for a long while, listening to the soft sounds of his breath move in and out, occasionally catching in a sigh and tiny swallowing sounds. When his breath stopped, I held mine and counted. *One, two, three.* Another moment, another breath, and I then began to trace rivers on his legs and paint imaginary pictures of mountains and moons and hearts and little boxes, but I soon shifted again, moving my head down to his toes, spending the night circling around him like a planet.

It had only been a day, but I realized then it had been the first day I hadn't done drugs for maybe ten years.

William left late the next afternoon. When the van pulled up and the little Mexican man wearing a Dodgers cap came to the door, I locked myself in the bathroom, refusing to help, refusing to say good-bye, but I watched him leave through the window and felt frightened as I saw him swallowed by the van's lift, the door shutting tight with a sucking sound. As they drove away, they became smaller and smaller, and I found myself wishing for a wave from the back window but remembered there would never be anything like that and how with William I only noticed the absence of such things.

When William left, life grew unbearably slow. During the days when I was home I lay on the floor, sensing time shift to hours, hours to minutes, then stopping to rest in tiny pulses as if it was running in place. My first project was devising grand, dramatic schemes of suicide in my head: death by drowning, death by bleeding, death by gas, placing the options in columns, listing advantages and disadvantages. I chose slitting my wrists as the best way to die, the most dramatic, and when I imagined myself dead in a bath of blood, I thought about how sad that would be, and when I felt that sadness in earnest, I began noticing things. Dust balls, and spiders, the color of green on the wings of an everyday housefly, and when they became dull, I studied the cracks on my ceiling, memorizing each one by heart, and though I was hoping to find pictures up there, I could find no interesting patterns. When I grew tired of that, I studied the sun, watching light fly through the windows, and over long stretches of time like this my schemes of suicide soon opened to theories about what traveled in the rays of the sun.

By then I knew that my life had become a game, a test of light and dark, of life and death, all those doors I traveled through late at night, the clicking and clacking of tiny metal tongues slipping in and out of their frames, locking and unlocking, opening and closing, and over time the person I was had grown small and ghostly, and I meet her again only in dreams, her face floating around my mind as I walk up and down the same hallway in and out of rooms and inside each room people like William. May. Josy. Lydia. A woman with an apricot pie. It was here that I first knew love and the difference between life and death, what is real and what is not.

"Rain is real," Josy had told me over a year ago. We were outside hiding in the shadows under a roof overhang. I looked beyond Josy and in the light saw the translucent sheen of rain. "It's real 'cause you can feel it on your skin.

"This bottle is real." Josy tapped a small vial of cocaine with her fingernail and pushed it up to her nose and snorted. I could hear the tiny tinking and the quick sucking sounds but couldn't see her face in the dark.

"The drug is real," she laughed. "But Hannah, hon, what it does to you makes you unreal, out of this world, not to be believed."

She shoved the bottle under my nose. "Shoot," she said. I snorted and within an instant felt the familiar burning and clearing of my mind. *Clean as a whistle*, I thought as I felt interesting thoughts pile up for processing. *Things are real, but thinking is not. There is no such thing as heaven or hell. Rivers are real, but love is not. Drugs are real, but I am not.*

It is autumn now and with this, the nights have grown long and cool, and when I lie here at night sometimes, I listen to the coyotes play tricks with their voices. I can never tell where they are exactly, and it makes me sad, the nature of things, how animals play tricks to kill, pushing their voices off of canyon walls to confuse their prey. No matter how much time goes by, when

I hear their calls, I feel fear, and when I feel fear, my heart does somersaults in my chest, and I think back to the days of drugs, the days of William beside me, knowing he could never feel that knock and whirl of the heart.

I know I am strange. I think very strange things all day long. When I stare out my windows sometimes, I see heaven, and from there I see the world wrapped in a tiny ball in William in the corner room of a blue cabin with white shutters, and from there I see rich, luscious valleys where rivers wind around the earth like candy ribbons, their banks crumbling and sweet as chocolate layer cake. From there I see everything there is to know.

In our strange months together, whenever I slept I dreamt I was blind, but now as I live and dream I see all the time, and if I fall into darkness, William is always near. "Hey, you," I say. "Tell me about the color blue. Remember me to the color of blue. Remember blue to me."

"What do you say? It's clear. It's melancholy, kind of sentimental and sad. You know faith. You know hope. That, my dear, is color. Blue, red, crimson, and yellow. It's all the same."

And as he talks I roll over with the phone in my ear and think about summertime, and how in the mornings when it rains hard like this, I love to lie in bed and think about stupid things: the rabbits eating my garden, the little girl next door who screams in my windows, *The magic never stops*, the UPS man who feeds the Mexicans at the corner in the mornings, and all the things I have come to know. And now as William sings "Row, Row, Row Your Boat" a little too dramatically I think, there is a small fat dog that lies on my feet, snoozing on his back, snoring and grunting, a lackadaisical paw in the air. Today is Monday. The painters are coming to paint the kitchen. Tomorrow is Tuesday. They will come again, arriving with their buckets of hope and color. When they knock, the dog will go "woof," but it will be such a sorry bark. He will be far too tired to get up and go to the door. I might, though. I might put this notebook aside, pull myself out of bed, pad to the door in my bare feet, smiling and sleepy, and say welcome to my world, I am nobody, but I am different from who I was.

These Hours

The way Louise saw it, Alain had died around
noon, but it wasn't until after midnight, a thousand minutes later,
when she realized she was alive and driving in a car by the sea
with a man she had met in a bar a week before. She had called the
man because she didn't want to be alone. Now they were driving
along the coast for what seemed like forever. They were taking
the long way to his place. A place somewhere in the San Fernando
Valley. A place where nothing ever happened. A city or town; she
hadn't bothered to ask its name.

She closed her eyes and felt the strangeness that had surrounded
her for hours seep deeper. It was a feeling of another world. She
could have been in Japan, for all she knew, but there she imagined

the mountains would be rounder, the water bluer, the air cooler to the skin. Here in Los Angeles life was different.

Louise turned toward the man, wanting to tell him about these differences, specifically about the ocean and how, depending on the weather, it changed color in the most dramatic and serious way. Oceans shouldn't do that, she wanted to say.

She was taking it personally.

He was Japanese.

She moved closer to smell him, a spicy pungent odor. He wore a bright white shirt unbuttoned at the collar and Levi jeans with buttons up the fly. His name was Ed, a poet, broad chested with a small bottom, dark and handsome in all the right ways.

He held the steering wheel with the tips of his fingers, his free arm wrapped around her shoulders.

"On good days when the ocean is green you can pretend you are anywhere," Louise said. "If we sliced tomatoes, got feta and retsina, and hung on the beach, it would *feel* like Greece. All we'd have to do is imagine the white stucco villages and the blue shutters. Isn't that strange how a mind can do that?"

"Yeah," he said, pulling her closer. "Tell me, Louise, where would you like to be? If you could be anywhere."

"Oh, I don't know," she said. "Here. There. It feels the same."

"Do you surf? Would you like to go surfing?"

"Good God, no," she said. "But I did once. I ate two hits of windowpane at Thanksgiving and went surfing in Santa Barbara. I surfed with Alain, the man who died today."

"How did you find it?" Ed asked.

Tripping or surfing? she thought.

"Inevitable." She sucked a breath. "It's not a quality thing."

She watched Ed closely and thought how he could have been anyone. He was round, not angular. He wore tinted glasses almost all the time. Did he sleep with his eyes open? She knew a man who did. She knew that this was a distinct possibility.

Louise didn't know when Jeffrey called, but he did call. "Hello, Louise," he said. "It's Jeffrey. Alain wanted me to call to tell you he died today." That is all. She sat on the floor and counted fingers.

themselves, he in the foreground, she just behind, with mountain peaks poking out of their heads.

As they drove over the pass to the Valley, Louise talked about Alain with the idea that if she talked about him, he wouldn't die in a big way. So he'd stay with her on some level.

"This is what the astronauts-who've-turned-Buddhist say," she said to Ed. "When friends die, they remain part of us. If we talk about them, they become part of others."

She told Ed about the last time she talked with Alain a month ago. The way he called and said, "Louise, it's me. I'm in Grenada. I'm in love and it's raining."

She also told Ed about Alain losing his money in the bars in Paris where he would go to get sucked off after dinner.

"The men who sucked his penis took all his money," she said. "He liked it. He must have because he always went back."

She didn't tell Ed everything. She didn't tell him that she was waiting for her dead friend to do something significant. She didn't tell him that she was afraid he wanted her to go with him.

"Oh," Ed said as he pulled her closer, pushing her hand onto his hard crotch. He knew he was going to slip it in. What he didn't know was that, like Alain, Louise had a fascination about strangers. She also had had a long-term goal to do a Japanese man ever since she saw a movie about Pearl Harbor and fell in love with the lead. *So there.*

Ed's house was in suburbia, dark under a grove of trees. He kissed her in the car. Big wet teasing kisses. He told her he was going to make her dessert in the nude and smear it all over her body.

"Then I'll lick it off."

"We can do anything."

"We can do it in the yard," he said.

Fifteen cracker boxes, different colors and medium sized, lined the counters in the kitchen. Layers of moist kitchen towels and dirty dishes were piled near the sink. The dark furniture was worn, with holes in its arms. The floors and ceilings were a mustard color with specks of olive. There was no art, no fireplace, no animals. It was cold even though the temperature was hovering in the nineties.

Ed opened the cognac and undressed Louise slowly as she watched herself in a mirror in between the gold splashes and crystal buttons holding it onto the wall. She felt cold sleeping with another stranger, seeking the attention of a man she could never really know, but this was her disease, and, watching Ed now, she knew he shared in this. He offered an éclair with his tongue and she sucked the pastry off. He whispered how he liked it, and the moments stretched long in their emptiness.

When the sun pushed itself above the horizon, Ed led Louise outside to the yard. It was a lovely place, with gardens full of flowers and vegetables surrounded by a wooden fence. They lay down and watched clouds move fitfully like dust.

"Look, Ed," she said, pointing to the sky, "there are dinosaurs."

Her back felt moist against the grass while she watched the clouds, but Ed suddenly didn't have time. He pulled her on top of him and pushed himself. Hard.

"Ouch," she said.

She rolled onto her back and closed her eyes. Even with her eyes closed she could make out the memory of a small patch of tomatoes and zucchinis in the side gardens where she and Ed lay. There were roses and pansies and gardenias, too.

"Look at me," he said, pulling her closer.

Eyes closed, she struggled out from underneath him, and, turning her back so it faced him as a pale and solid wall, she wrapped her arms around herself, rocking forward and back, and recounted the garden's fruits. Fifteen tomatoes. Ten zucchinis. Five roses. Three gardenia blossoms she could smell. She heard Ed call her but nothing else for a long time. Her own breath, perhaps, as the hours began melting again, and then, finally, Alain. He was reading a passage about a woman who put her ear to the sea and became whole. He was alive when he read her this. They were in an airport, maybe a year ago.

Arts and
Crafts of
American
WASPs

Mostly it's cable-knit sweaters. Pullovers and cardigans in pale and dark colors. Yellows, navy blues, and tans. Exotic wools from lambs and cashmere and sometimes a silk something knit on colored knitting needles as small as pins.

I've found these things in a cedar chest sent by my mother, and as I lift her old yellow sweater with round woolen buttons to my cheek, I see her as she slept maybe thirty years ago on a plum davenport in a room crafted of a special pine. In the corner of the room I remember a Franklin woodstove with brass knobs that now lies at the bottom of my driveway, too heavy for anyone to lift, and as I rummage through the chest, pulling out quilts and embroidered pillowcases, I try again to re-create the room where my mother slept. There was a bank of windows behind the couch, but it wasn't the room I had imagined a moment before. The davenport and the stove were in a glass porch of my grandmother's home. The home I grew up in is empty, and though I can see my mother sleeping, her face is washed out, and I no longer know what was there. I walk through the objects that I had the moving men put out in the barn and hunt for the things that connect me.

What is a mother?

I've bought an ovulation kit to test the possibilities.

In the kit are six plastic cups, six droppers, and six foil pouches containing test cassettes, each with a urine well and a window in which to read test results.

If I do not detect a surge after testing, the instructions state, if my cycle is irregular or if for any other reason I do not detect a surge after testing, I am instructed to call the doctor or the Technical Assistance Line.

My mother has sent me her life in boxes and pieces of old wood and I study these like artifacts. In the cedar chest, kerchiefs and sweaters, woolen scarves and hats, books by Emily Post and Amy Vanderbilt, knitting and needlepoint bags full of my grandmother's half-finished embroidery, letters, and old stationery. A family of broken arrow-back chairs, paintings and boxes, photographs, a pine table or two from a lake home long forgotten. My great-grandfather's desk, paintings. Bureaus. Blanket chests. Embroidered sayings. Grandmother's recipes for Parker House rolls and plum pudding. A cobbler's bench. A blacksmith's nail carrier. A hand-painted writing desk. Afghans purchased at the church bazaar. Finger paintings. Sculptures. Braided reins. Spindle spool beds, golden treasures, and charm bracelets. Rocking chairs. Diamond watches, platinum rings, and my mother's silver.

I cannot place these objects.

A mother is a memory of something sweet.

The test tells me it is fast, accurate, and easy to use. It predicts possibilities in hormonal surges; the surging of hormones means this: the luteinizing hormone climbs through secret places and makes things happen. Little people come to life. They come to expect it.

I call my mother in Florida to let her know that everything had arrived, and her voice closes around me like a sacrifice. My father had died six months before, and within this time she had sold the house and moved to their winter home in Florida, and now she was sending these precious family things all the way to California; she had hired big men to package and assemble and sign away all that she wore or sat upon or gazed at. I wind through these objects, and fragments float back as if unearthed from an ancient sleep. "These are yours now," my mother had said. "Take care of them."

The barn where my mother and father's life rests in piles is fifty-five paces from my front door down a series of wooden steps that weave through a garden. I stand in the center surrounded by my parents' things and work on this image of my sleeping mother, attempting to paint in and around the spaces of long afternoons, watching her sleep, but I transpose the objects from other rooms from neighbors and friends and grandparents, so the room remains empty, and my mother is in a heap like broken glass. I pull her toward me, measuring her breath in numbers and ABCs. She looks strangely serene, nestled on a bed of my father's overcoats that smell vaguely of him; of Old Spice and cigarettes in hard red boxes. I climb on top of her and stick my fingers in her mouth and count teeth. I pull out her tongue and hide it in my hand like a secret. Years later when this tongue talks to me, I see it clearly and wonder if I could count the hours I lay looking at it, holding it in between my fingers, folding it over itself, memorizing the map of veins on its back.

"I am sorry," my mother says, "I am overcome by remorse."

If someone makes a gift of their remorse, how does one express their feelings of thanks? I leaf through books for answers.

THE THANK YOU LETTER
A child should send thank you notes to thank for presents, parties attended, and having been asked to spend the night. If a child forms this habit early, he will carry it through his life and will find good manners will always be one of his greatest assets.

Dear Mother,
Many thanks for your remorse. I have wrapped it hand-somely and placed it on the mantle underneath the photo-graph of your mother's brother, Fearman. John enjoys the remorse, too. We sat with it on Saturday.
With love,
Michelle

Early that morning, I peed in a plastic cup. I am testing possibilities of a role I cannot define or remember. I draw my urine, and it feels anxious at its possibilities. The possibilities are endless. I am testing the levels of hormones that evaluate my possibilities as a mother. I am looking into this role as mother; it is a possibility, and like anyone I look to my mother for guidance, and I cannot find her. My mother is lost among her things. I look for her under tables and in drawers.

If I were to reach deep into my self, would I find a uterus shaped like a pear? And if I found this, what then?

The pamphlet tells me that ovulation is a possibility; it is the release of an egg from my ovary. It says that it is important to know that the LH surge and ovulation may not occur in all cycles. It does not say why or why not. It does not say anything else.

If I am unsure about my usual cycle length, I am told to use the shortest cycle length when reading the WHEN TO START CHART. If I have questions about my cycle or if my cycle is not shown on the chart, I am instructed to call 1-800-874-1517 (toll-free) for assistance.

I walk back to the house with more boxes, and when I see the antique stove, it looks small and forgotten. I walk around it and place my hand against the hard black steel to feel for the crack in the cast iron. My mother's father, a man I came to know as cruel and impatient, burned coal instead of wood, and the stove grew too hot and cracked in half. I sit on top of it. The metal feels solid and dark, and I move my fingers down its back, hunting its surface for clues, and am relieved somehow when I feel the uneven metal. I consider the possibility. I consider the possibility of a truth; a crack is here, and I see it as certainty. I move around the stove and kneel down to get a better look, measuring the length of its scar with my hand. I am looking for truth. How does one measure it? How does one know how to measure a truth? I see all these truths, whole truths and half-truths. They all sit together and talk about things. Truths conspire. They connect. Phantom rooms fill and empty at a whim. Photographs and a cuckoo clock, a cobbler's bench, a rose-colored-velvet-covered rocking chair, a blanket chest that smells of ginger ale, and a funny story from an old man, who told me about kissing meter maids in downtown Boston. "They kiss you to see if you've been drinking," my grandfather says, his top teeth falling to the bottom of his mouth. "They kiss you to smell your breath."

I am considering the possibilities. Mother hen. Mother superior. Mother Hubbard. Motherhouse. Motherfucker. Mother figure. Mother Goose. Mother lode.

How important is timing?

Can I store my urine and test later?

What happens if I see the line grow darker than the reference line?

At the bottom of the cedar chest I find scarves, hats, and mittens with snowflake patterns knitted in happy colors, and when I hold them to my face, I expect things. I gather the woolens, placing the hand-knitted mittens on my hands, and stretch out in a band of light on the bedroom floor. As a child, I had watched other mothers knit these things for their daughters as gifts, and I remember marveling at these mothers as masterpieces, their hands, their long spindly fingers that knew things, these beautiful fingers that wrapped the woolen crafts around girly faces and then stepped back to admire their work.

"Michelle," my friend Judith's mother said. "I made you a hat in blue." I looked at her, and she held out a hat for me, and I instinctively stepped forward and bent my head down for her to tie it on as she had done minutes before for her own daughter. "And mittens . . . Here, give me your jacket." She took a mitten and, like a needle and thread, weaved it through the arms of my red winter jacket. She sewed me together with a pair of mittens connected by a string of yarn. She motioned for me to turn around, and when I did she guided my hands into the arms of my jacket. She stepped back, and Judith and I stood together. "You two," she said. "Cute as buttons."

I am wearing these mittens on my hands. I am testing the possibilities. My hands are loyal. They hang at my sides. I talk to my hands. I study them. I have often turned to my hands for advice. I ask them about their lives; I ask them, Are you the kinds of hands that could ever see themselves as a mother?

I am my mother and we are sleeping.

I climb into her and float. I hold my breasts and feel my ribs. My mother is sleeping on the floor of the dining room in the afternoon, and I do the same, not because I am drunk but because I am sad. This is a sadness that wears on me. So, rather than carry it always, I lie down in the bands of light in different rooms and let it carry me. I have moved now from the bedroom to the dining room. I am looking for my mother. I study the things I've made or collected from strangers as if they unlock the secrets that I seem to hold so dear.

Landscapes and seascapes in thick, dark, sad gobs of colors lit by small special brass lamps with little black buttons with fluorescent bulbs shaped like hot dogs. When I visited with my grandparents, I saw similar paintings and wanted to eat them, throw the paint around my body so I could live inside. I touched every part of them with my fingers. Every painting in the house. I stood on chairs and went from top to bottom, room to room, moving down to the smaller paintings of flowers pinned along the long halls that wound through three stories, a home with green shutters and latticework. It was open and airy; ivory rooms with lace and flowered-curtained bay windows and window seats made of old wood with Navaho rugs on the hardwood floors.

I had talked to my hands. My hands and I had made assumptions. We assumed these were the things that my mother had touched when she was a child.

I find a map of metropolitan Boston and follow the highway to my home. The house is red but it is empty, and inside I find my mother sleeping. I climb on top of her, afraid that she will die. I push my fingers in her nose to stop her breath. Her chest rises and stops, and I hold my fingers there until I feel her stir, a tension in her body beneath me, a body hungry for breath. I am waiting for a breath. I am waiting for my mother to open her mouth. I let go and turn to face the room and listen. I am thinking little girl thoughts. I am thinking about breath.

I am looking for a hormonal surge to test the possibilities. The possibilities are endless. I can work in a bank. I can be a doctor, a lawyer, a CEO.

Some etiquette expert wrote: A revolution in the social mores of business has occurred. There is a new world, with women attempting to gain equal footing with the traditional keepers of the corporate and professional keys—men. Yet many women are unsure. Something had to emerge.

Dear Mother:
Many thanks for the anxiety. It fits so well alongside the remorse, which I have placed in pretty blue bottles bought by Grandmother in Europe. Did she purchase them at Fauchon in Paris? I have placed the ambivalence in the willow vase, which is in the window facing south. John enjoys these

things, too. We have been busy looking for esteem for me
to wear along with those pretty kerchiefs; I think it could be
stunning beside the desperation.
   With love,
   Michelle

On the wall I see my grandmother's embroidered saying stitched in rainbow colors on faded and stained Irish linen. "If I should pass this way once, let me show kindness, for I shall never pass this way again" hung in a dark wood frame, sealed behind cool glass so I couldn't touch it or feel the texture. These are the things the women in my family pass on to me. This hangs now over a bureau in our dining room in California and was made by my father's mother, and its placement in my life now is just as strange as anything. I am under the table in the dining room looking for my mother. I am looking for my mother so I might test the possibilities. My mother isn't breathing, and because of this I find myself holding my breath—waiting. I hear my husband moving around our house. "Honey?" he says. He is standing in the doorway between the dining and living room and I am under the table, and as I reach for some explanation, he turns away.

I must have fallen asleep.

On the floor?

Yes, I'm afraid so.

All my parents' things are here. Do you want to see?

My instructions are as follows:
1. Remove the test cassette from the foil pouch and place it on a flat, dry surface.
2. Place the dropper in the urine sample. Draw urine into the dropper.
3. Hold the urine dropper upright about half an inch above the urine well at the bottom of the test cassette.
4. Add only three drops of urine to the urine well.
5. Wait three minutes and then read your test result.

As a child I dreamt of people in the downstairs sitting room at cocktail hour. The women wore their hair in flips and had peach lipstick on their lips. The men dressed in dark blue blazers and had paisley bow ties around their necks. The ladies dressed in pink and green dresses with sagging bows at the collars. These women's hands fiddled with the bows at their collars as the men played with the change in their front pockets and talked about the stock market and fine art, sipping martinis and smoking cigarettes while sitting on ancestral antiques from Europe and elsewhere.

The hutch was given by a grand-uncle in France. A man in the country of Vermont built the butler table. It was built with his two hands. This is my father speaking as he holds a martini made with elegant British gin. *Men love a woman who knows how to make a good martini,* he tells me. *Put the ice in the cocktail shaker. Pour in the gin. Now watch me, Michelle, this is very important. Wave the bottle of vermouth over the shaker. Only wave,* he laughs. *Don't pour any in. The Wellingtons like their martinis dry. Isn't that right, my girl?*

My husband sleeps holding his hands like a corpse. I climb on top of him and hold him. His breath is steady. I am digging in my mind. I am digging up gardens. I am pulling the gardens up by the roots. I move out of bed gently and pad through the house in the dark.

In the barn, in the middle of the night, I walk around and touch everything my mother has sent me. I pull open all the drawers. I rearrange piles. I am looking for possibilities. I juxtapose objects like truths. I place objects outside, upside down, in opposite corners, and I lie down. The house is empty. I am very small. I hold my mother's eyes open with my fingers, one by one. Left. Right. Then both at the same time, and I see her looking at me, but I suspect that she is not there. I climb into her. I am looking out. I can feel the folds in her skin, the dead weight of her body sleeping.

Needlepoint pillows. Landscape paintings. Quilts in blue and red hang on the four-poster beds in the spare bedrooms. Yorkshire pudding, hollandaise, baked Alaska, peach cobbler, roast pork, shepherd's pie, coq au vin. Two eggs, two cups of sugar, one cup of flowers. Waltzes and fox-trots.

These are the things my mother has sent me. They have been passed down for generations. In the morning, I will pee in a plastic cup and study the hues of blue. The pink-to-purple test line must be darker than the reference line. It's important to remember that no matter how many days I have these surges, the first day and the next day and a half are the days, the pamphlet says, the ones; these are the best times to make the baby. After each test I must decide.

Avalanche!

(a fairy tale)

———

After lunch Isabel watched Lucy paint her lips in the mirror. Lucy first rested a hand on her collarbone and stared at herself as if in disbelief. She then curled her fingers around a lip pencil; her silver-coated fingernails fanned into the form of a strange winged bird and floated toward Lucy's lips in slow motion. Isabel imagined a propeller, a piece of candy or bone, and realized again how captivating these rituals were in a place where women reinvented themselves weekly.

It was here in this very ladies' room that Isabel first learned about thongs before they were cool, how certain hemorrhoid creams could be used to plump wrinkles around the eye and mouth, as well as Jackie O's secret moisturizing formula using

Crisco. After learning these tricks, Isabel could not help but assume an anthropological eye on these ladies because their beauty routines were so very innovative—and, well, so very astonishing. Most had acquired the latest gadgets and potions and spent inordinate amounts of time mastering the most mundane beauty tasks directed, of course, by the whims of movie stars, who floated around town like tiny exploding constellations.

As a girl who grew up on a dairy farm in Vermont the whole *paint your face shebang* had always mystified Isabel. Even at the age of thirty-five, the process seemed fraudulent, as if the painting of a mask made her more unrecognizable to herself than she already was. Nevertheless, she had spent her life going through the paces, like now, watching Lucy Hernandez in the mirror, Lucy bent over the black granite sink, her face so close that her breath appeared on the glass as she smeared lip liner the color of baby poop around the perimeter of her lips.

Behind Lucy's reflection Isabel saw her own image surrounded by tiny glittering globes of light. Isabel had never felt she actually inhabited this image but rather stood outside looking in. Like now, she watched herself dig through her bag and pluck out a lipstick that was embedded in a piece of gum from the bottom, and then she froze momentarily, reminding herself to breathe slowly as the doctor had instructed her to match the hollow rhythm of her rolling heart: *In, one-two-three; out, one-two-three.*

"Breathing is good," the doctor had said. "Isabel Babbitt, you must remember to breathe." He had instructed her to breathe slowly and deeply, particularly in the middle of the night, when she often awoke locked in a swirl of a dream, suffocating, her body desperate for breath, her lungs frozen until she opened her eyes and reminded herself: *Breathe!* For the rest of the night she lay in a blue-black darkness, sorting her mind for the invisible thing that was keeping her from breathing, the invisible thing about not wanting to swallow, the invisible thing telling her body there was some reason not to breathe.

The truth was that Lucy Hernandez had always fascinated Isabel because Lucy was beautiful in a luminescent, shimmery way, and it was a beauty that transported her to places Isabel would never go. The most interesting at the moment was that Lucy had gone home with Jack Nicholson a few nights before. But long before that, Lucy Hernandez had once been married to one of the brothers of The Most Famous Pop Star in the Universe and when she was only thirteen had also had an affair with a rock and roll star and his son—simultaneously. It was all this that captivated Isabel, plus the endless gossip Lucy recounted in her deep, throaty voice about celebrity outings, and *Vanity Fair* columnists, various movie stars' penis sizes, and love techniques—or lack of—that was enough to keep Isabel sufficiently distracted so she never had to think about anything but the consuming, exhausting tidbits of shiny people's lives. In the case of Lucy's ex-husband, who wasn't *as* famous, of course, as The Most Famous Pop Star in the Universe but was, rather, the one with the bad hairdo on *American Bandstand*, the one into drugs who lived in the family castle in the San Fernando Valley, and the one who was so weird and violent one year before that Lucy had to flee the castle in the middle of the night. She fled because he had set her hair on fire with a small blowtorch used for smoking cocaine. She had lost all of it on the right, from the part to the tips of the falling cascade, so she had to leave the castle with half a head of hair and walk all the way down the curvy wooded driveway into the city on Ventura Boulevard with suitcases and her two young sons. All of it, the hair, the songs, the record labels, the lovers, the drugs, the story of her life on the streets as a teenage runaway, were in Lucy's new book that Isabel had just finished editing called *A Pop Star's Family Values.*

Unfortunately, even though Isabel knew practically every secret this woman ever had, she had yet to crack the story about going home with Jack Nicholson, and Isabel had actually met the man in an elevator in the Sunset Building on her way to see the gynecologist a few years before. She had met him at a particular low point in her life, three weeks after her husband, Billy, had been reported missing helicopter snowboarding in Alaska, one week following her return from the avalanche search-and-rescue attempts where she watched many men poke the snow with long rods. They had spent days hunting for Billy's body until it was clear that the other avalanche, the second avalanche that buried their other friend, Clarke, made it impossible and too dangerous for anyone to continue.

When she stepped into the elevator, at first Isabel didn't notice anyone standing there. She was too busy staring at her shoes and crying, trying to prevent a complete meltdown, which she found herself doing in public at odd moments everywhere. When she looked up, wiping tears from her face, there stood a man who looked familiar, and he smiled at her, not in a special way but in a courteous way.

"Well, hello to you, too," he said.

She stepped back, lifted her hand to secure a strand of hair behind her ear, and turned away. "Sorry," she said, and in an instant it occurred to her that this man standing in front of her was Jack Nicholson.

The elevator stopped. The doors slid open to reveal several women's faces waiting.

"Going down?" one asked.

Nicholson pointed his thumb up and pressed the close door button. During the moment before the doors closed, Isabel saw the women's eyes light up, *Wait!* But it was too late. The doors sucked shut, and the silvery box floated toward the earth humming.

"They will all be so sad now," Isabel said. "How sad? They almost got to ride with the movie star Jack Nicholson."

He laughed and reached for her hand to give it an appreciative squeeze and held it for a moment before he let go. And then he removed his sunglasses and looked at her and, seeing that she had been crying, took her hand again. Isabel, face red and eyes swollen, placed her other hand over her heart and feigned a swoon. He then hugged her and said, "I'm sorry."

That was the extent of it, and though it happened three years before, she had replayed the moment at least a million times. She had spent the three weeks before consumed by high-pitched hysteria and dread while standing in the cold, watching men and dogs search for her buried husband. During that time, no matter where she would go she remained *Standing There*, her heart frozen still in a restricted territory, on a mountain the name of which she couldn't pronounce, on a glacier she had hoped would open and deliver her husband of six years. Jack Nicholson's random kindness reminded her of magical things, of fate and possibilities, specifically, the possibility of her husband being found alive. It was in that nanosecond of humanity from a stranger, his funny sort of smile and eyebrow thing, that she knew, even though Billy's friend Charles kept calling and trying to prepare her for the worst, she knew Billy's beacon was still beeping, and if she could share an encouraging moment like this, it might still be possible for Billy to come home.

He never did, although she often dreamt that he did. And oddly, when Billy first came to her in sleep he looked like Jack Nicholson. During the first year following his accident, Billy's best friend, Charles, the only survivor on the trip, had stayed with her to help her get back on her feet. She often found herself up in the middle of the night sitting at the end of Charles's bed filled with extravagant hope. As she would always tell Charles, in the dream she had been digging for days, and by the time she was able to finally unearth Billy, he was Jack Nicholson and smiling like he did with Candy Bergman in *Carnal Knowledge*. But when Isabel began to speak and clear the snow away, Jack's face turned to Billy's face, a sleepy face as if he had just woken from a nap, his eyes still squished in dream.

Charles would lie perfectly still, waiting for her to stop talking, and then slide his arms around her. She could feel his body heave as if he was in midair and had encountered turbulence, and she had reminded herself that he was the one who had watched Billy and Clarke surf the slab of snow before they vanished. He was the one who had been able to pull Clarke from the edge of the slide and watch him die before the rest of the mountain came down, burying Billy so deep and making the area so unstable that no probe could ever reach him. Night after night, holding on to each other, Isabel found herself immersed in the details of Charles's face. He had almond-shaped green eyes, cheekbones like baby apples, and bad acne scars around the line of his jaw.

She awoke slowly those mornings of that first year, lollygagging in the twilight, seconds between sleep and consciousness, knowing the hazy truth lay in wait. In that brief second of levity, she was able to not dwell in the loss but rather pondered the curiosity of Jack Nicholson's role. A moment later, a fog of sadness covered her in a blanket of all things of Billy. She wrapped him around her and spent day after day watching him spring to life as they traveled through the years, through an ivory darkness from Boston to Los Angeles, wandering knee-deep in a streambed headed for a swim in the waterfall upstream. On these adventures of memory it was always raining and Billy hummed as he walked, splashing in the water, holding out his hands, making invisible boxes out of thin air. *Can you feel it? Isabel, can you feel the air? It has shape.* She followed him, trying to imagine it, feeling the air, feeling its shape as she pulled plants from their path and the sweet aroma of sage and eucalyptus exploded from her fingertips. After some time Billy would vanish and reappear standing on a rock or in a tree and yell *I love you, Is, I love you Is, I love Is,* at the top of his lungs and she laughed because he made his voice sound high and funny, and she laughed because their lives felt swollen with possibility, and luck, and love.

Isabel knew it was not a happy thing that within a month of his disappearance she had transferred her sadness into longing for a movie star and some days felt quite, what was the word her shrink had used? *Pathological?* But no matter what she made up or what books she wrote for movie stars and producers and the people who knew them, she couldn't resurrect that part of her still frozen and breathless on an Alaskan glacier, watching men and dogs run around probing for bodies in the snow.

Like now, while watching Lucy's postlunch primp in the mirror, Isabel found herself unable to move. She stood frozen as if she was waist-deep in a drift of snow instead of in Beverly Hills looking into the perplexed eyes of Lucy Hernandez.

"Are you okay?" Lucy had asked Isabel.

"Of course." Isabel smiled and then stepped back from the mirror to assume her *deer in the headlight* look to discover that somehow her pink lip liner had strayed way off her lip as if on the path of a wild pony. She looked again and saw Lucy behind her, smiling beautifully, heart-stopping drop-dead gorgeous. Isabel, though beautiful in a simple way, was not heart stopping that, but a plain girl with freckles and hazel eyes, no boobs, and who, sadly, never married or divorced or fucked anybody known for anything even remotely interesting other than minor traffic violations, losing at pool, and dying young. Not that anyone would know this, since, with the exception of Lucy, she had never mentioned what happened to the man who was attached to the beautiful emerald ring she wore around her neck. She thought about it. What could she say, really? *Oh, by the way, I had a husband. He was a researcher at UCLA. And only a year after moving here he disappeared in an avalanche in Alaska and we never found his body. He became a glacier, and people probably ski over him.* For people in Los Angeles avalanches were titles of movies followed by exclamation points! Not things that actually ever happened!

Isabel smiled a toothy grin, revealing an incisor smothered in shocking pink lip liner. *Screw it,* she thought and wiped the back of her hand across her lips. Lucy laughed and threw her arms around Isabel. "You are so adorable! Really! So down to earth!" Isabel smiled and then patted Lucy's shoulder uncomfortably to push her away and walked out of the bathroom through the window-lined hallways of a publishing company that catered to movie stars and All Things Los Angeles.

Isabel felt like she had swallowed an atom bomb. Before she had landed in the ladies' room with Lucy she had eaten too much squid risotto while lunching with The Best Friend of the Woman Murdered by the Famous Football Star. They had sat outside in a courtyard of glass full of glass tables and beautiful people drinking bubbly water and smoking brown cigarettes. Isabel appeared to be the only one eating, and because she was nervous about everything in general, she ate until she felt like she might pop. She was trying to remain attentive listening to the tales of The Best Friend of the Woman Murdered by the Famous Football Star, who had just returned from a trip that included but was not limited to being held up at the Plaza in the city wearing cheap sunglasses while trying to avoid Johnny Cochran's hit squads after being deposed in the famous football star's wrongful death suit, all the while desperately trying to catch a plane to Paris.

Isabel laughed when she heard the part about "trying to catch a plane to Paris" because no matter how dramatic this woman sounded, her life still fell into a pillow of privilege. Everyone in the restaurant turned around in their seats and scowled. "I cannot believe you did that," the woman whispered. "I am sooooo embarrassed."

Why, Isabel thought. *All I did was laugh.*

The woman glared, stabbing at her black-and-white penne with her fork, and continued. Isabel watched, mesmerized by the woman's skin and hair that appeared to be spun out of gold. Her eyes were the color of nut berries, with orange and yellow freckles like marmalade, and, like Lucy, The Best Friend of the Woman Murdered by the Famous Football Star also loved Isabel. She had told her that she thought Isabel was a woman's woman, a savior, an angel! Isabel smiled as she heard this, trying to understand how these compliments might sink in, when all she could manage was to watch them sail by like volleyballs.

What she wanted to do was tell these ladies how it felt to have someone you love buried alive. What she wanted to do was stand on chairs and reel off the statistics of and rescue strategies for avalanche victims, which she had stayed up and read one night:

Where was the last-seen area?
Where was the person's entry point into the slide?
Was there a witness?
Are there any surface clues?
Everyone should now switch his or her beacons to receive,
and the search should begin. Once you've picked up a signal,
send more searchers to the area. Clear the victim's head first.

What Isabel had intended for her life was quite different, was, in fact, she believed, even noble. She wanted to deliver babies. In college she founded a student health collective and, with a speculum, a mirror, and a flashlight, showed all the women— hundreds of them—on campus their cervix. For some reason, and she really could not understand now ten years later, it was exciting to see what went on up there. One night she brought her collective to see a grainy black-and-white documentary about the underground woman's movement, hosted by a woman who weighed four hundred pounds who was showing women cervixes on film. One of Isabel's little friends leaned over. "That's going to be you one day."

She didn't mean to imply the fat part, but that's how Isabel saw it.

Isabel smiled, said nothing, but made the decision on the spot. *No. I don't think so.* And that was the end of the cervix-showing days.

Her mother was always aghast. "Whatever the hell that was about, I'll never know." She called it Isabel's pink period, but Isabel thought of it as blue, the cervix-showing era, the time just before she met and fell in love with Billy.

She had seen him a million times passing in the hallways at work, but she silently watched him pass by until very late one night in the middle of a snowstorm in the center of a park near Harvard Square. She was returning from a late movie and found him standing under a streetlight studying the palm of his hand.

"How many do you think?" he asked her when she walked by.

"How many?" she asked.

"Yeah, Miss Isabel Babbitt, if the air is composed of oxygen and nitrogen and carbon dioxide, and if one oxygen molecule measures a millionth of a micrometer, how many oxygen molecules will float on the palm of a hand?"

"How do you know my name?"

"How?" he said, teasing. "Magic."

She stood speechless, staring into his hand, and he began to laugh, touching her ever so lightly on the small of her back.

"It was a joke," he said.

The year of the health collective, the year of meeting Billy, was the year Isabel started taking writing classes but also worked part-time cutting up placentas at the medical school downtown, slicing sections that looked like little chicken parts, creating cellular transport vessels to test how glucose passed through cells. Billy, who had just graduated from medical school, was doing a residency in cardiology while also working on a Ph.D. in public health. Before they met in the snow they had been bumping into each other in the elevator, Isabel with her bucket of placentas that the delivery nurses saved for her at the start of each week. Her cheeks were always flushed from the excitement in Labor and Delivery, the bright lights and all the beaming baby bodies in the nursery, their strange, stunned little eyes and tiny fingers fanned out like little hors d'oeuvres.

By the time Isabel arrived back at her office, all the sharp edges of despair had settled in. She was lonely. She couldn't think of one person who actually knew her. Three years after Billy's disappearance she could barely remember her life with him. And after all this time she was still no one. Not only a big fat no one, but, as her psychiatrist had pointed out numerous times, she was also a no one with a fascination with celebrity, a pathological no one prone to long bouts of magical thinking. The shrink enunciated the sharp consonants of the K sounds of magical thinking as if daydreaming was a disease. "Good gracious," she had said, "a life philosophy does need to move beyond *Dear God, I want a pony.*"

"But how?" Isabel asked. "How?"

Isabel reached up and unbuttoned the top button on her pants and moved into her office to listen to messages and then sat down and placed her head on her desk and looked out the window through the courtyard to the gold script lettering across the street that read *Thrifty of Beverly Hills.* She did not want to listen to any more messages. Charles had already called several times over the past few days and left word from Turnigan Arm, another cheery adventure spot in Alaska where people get sucked into the sea floor by quicksand when the tide goes out. He was on a story assignment with a surf magazine, and he had news of some kind about Billy. He was speaking vaguely in the messages that Isabel had listened to earlier, but she had hung up when she heard "long summer" and "Billy," uncertain if it was news she wanted to know. She had been avoiding all of it, and Charles especially, not because she didn't love him, she did, but because they had fallen into a romantic thing and had been sleeping together, and three months ago she called it off.

"I don't love you," she told Charles. "I can't love you. You're Billy's best friend."

He rolled on top of her and covered her eyes with his hand.

"I don't believe you," he said.

"It's impossible," she continued. "You might as well return to the great Northwest Territories."

She lay there with her eyes closed.

"Isabel," Charles said. "This is the last time I will ask. There is nothing here for you anymore."

That was not true, for Isabel had changed nothing since Billy had died. He was everywhere in the little cabin they shared in the mountains outside Los Angeles.

"I am not sustainable," she said.

Charles was a commercial airplane pilot and into sustainable things, building green, living green, minimizing carbon dioxide emissions. He was 6' 4" but liked little things: Isabel and little planes that he barely fit into but insisted on flying on dangerous missions through Alaska and Baja Mexico. He did this for fun.

"I am unmaintainable," she said. "I am the opposite of green. I am blue."

"Not opposite," Charles said. "Just not at all."

That was three months earlier, and she hadn't seen him since. She missed him, but every time he called, she hung up. And finally he stopped. And now everything was gone. She hadn't known she was doing that, purging herself of him, but that is exactly what she has done, systematically dismantled her life, one person after another. Everything alive connected to Billy was now gone.

Her first purge was leaving science altogether; she left her job as an assistant editor at the *Journal of Clinical Psychopharmacology* and found a job as an assistant editor making celebrity books. It was a world Billy would loathe, which meant it was deliciously fun and distracting after proofreading papers on potassium levels. But after three years of being surrounded by people bleaching their teeth for book tours, it ceased to be fun. At least potassium was real. At least scientists' teeth did not resemble porcelain dinner plates. These days she felt like a stable hand, and her job was simply shoveling shit; she was surrounded by it. Like now, mountains of perfectly meaningless bullshit towered around her—stacks of books to be edited, books to be written, stories that had to be told. There were infinite numbers of *tell-alls* and *tell-abouts*: the forsaken and the fallen, the betrothed and the ballin'. Movie stars. Psychics. Transients. Doppelgangers. Whores. Ex-lovers. Wives. Pop stars. Producers. Pornographers. And pooches. No matter where she looked, there were only these silly scandalous stories about beautiful people who create and overcome tragedies like in fairy tales. And Isabel's life was not that. Her life was buried in

Alaska. Her life stopped in midair. Everything she once held dear was now far away.

She tried to return a few calls but was feeling jump-out-of-her-skin disagreeable. She wandered down the hall to the lawyer's office and threw herself into the chair in front of his desk. No matter how he tried, the man always appeared like a twelve year old in grown-up clothing. He didn't iron his shirts, so the shirt collars curled at the ends. He did not look up but kept typing.

"C'mon," she said, pushing again for what Lucy had said about her night with Jack Nicholson.

"No."

"I told you."

"I promised her."

"There are no secrets," she said. "C'mon. I told you about the producer and all the wives of world leaders."

"It didn't count," he said. "It was coming out anyway.

"Oh God," he said. "Forget it. It's true love. Nothing happened."

"Right," Isabel said. "Okay, when you're hot for a big piece of gossip . . ."

"Truly," he said. "Nothing. They talked."

Isabel stood and shut the door. "You have to tell me." She placed her hands on her ears and squished her face into the center so her lips turned inside out. She pushed out the underside of her tongue.

The buzzer sounded, and Lucy the receptionist came on in Spanish.

"Strange-looking man here who says he has a meeting with you and Isabel."

"Yes, it's true," the lawyer answered, also in Spanish. "We'll take it in here."

Isabel hated him. Not only was he a tennis star when he was sixteen, but he spoke Spanish and French fluently.

"He's wearing a trench coat," Lucy whispered. "It's 150 outside. And Isabel, Charles called. Again."

Isabel put a magazine over her face.

"It's the boyfriend of the DA who allegedly ran off with the very famous author," the lawyer said.

"No," Isabel whispered very loudly. *"It cannot be true."*

Lucy repeated, "Charles? Isabel?"

"Take a message," Isabel said.

"Who is Charles?" the lawyer asked.

"My dead husband's best friend."

"Very funny," he said.

"It's true," she said.

The lawyer shot her a searchless look and left the room to greet the man who was peddling the titillating story about the famous author.

The first thing the man told the lawyer and Isabel was that he was in the garbage business. At that moment Isabel knew she had seen too many *Godfather* movies, because she immediately saw a misty alley lined with dumpsters lit by a whole line of streetlights and three black Cadillacs parked head to toe. She rapidly pressed her fingers into her trousers. The lawyer was sitting across from her and was lifting his eyebrows at her finger pressing. He thought she was flirting, but she had none of those feelings. She pressed her trousers because she really had too much at lunch and was trying to stay awake.

The man was small, wore a mullet hairdo, and was slightly balding on top. He was what Isabel called a swinging dick, denoting how he swiggled, swaggered, and did everything but pick the damn thing up and shake it at her.

"So, they're carrying on and I don't know it," the man said. "It's all happening on the Internet, sending those notes back and forth. She meets him and comes home one day and says she's fucking leaving. Kaput."

"Leaving?" Isabel said.

"She was really something," he said, and then he wiggled, nodded, and moved his right hand quickly and blew on it a few times like he was trying to cool off something too hot. "Never fucking stopped. She kept right on coming." He laughed and wiggled in his chair, pathetically feigning a woman's orgasm like men so often do and fail at.

"Going. Whatever, dear," Isabel admonished him. "You don't need to go into great detail. We do have sex in L.A."

He laughed. And the lawyer rolled his eyes.

"You seem like a smart woman," he said and gave her arm a little pat, knocking it off the armrest. She returned her hand to the rest, curled her fingers, her knuckles whitening from the lack of blood, her tiny hands knotted into a death grip.

"So what?" Isabel said. "Who cares? I'm sure Mister X runs with women all the time."

"Well," he began to whisper, "when she left, she left in quite a hurry. She left her computer with all the love notes."

Isabel was silent. She looked at the lawyer and back at the man.

"Wow, now that is dumb," she said.

"Exactly," the man said, looking quickly at both the lawyer and Isabel as if he had said too much and suddenly wanted to take it all back.

The lawyer had been uncharacteristically quiet. "The thing that bothers me is she is a district attorney," the lawyer finally said.

"How long did it go on?" Isabel asked. "How many letters?"

"About six months," the man said. His feet and his head wiggled just slightly before his breath caught and his voice began to squeak. He stopped, lowered his head, and stared at his lap, and she knew he was struggling not to cry.

"I'm sorry," she said. "That's a terrible story."

The lawyer made a face, interrupting her. "But we need the letters before we can make a decision," he said, "so once you get that together, give us a call."

After the man left the lawyer accused Isabel of flirting, which she wasn't. "I was being friendly," she said. "I was showing compassion."

She spelled it out for him. "C-O-M-P-A-S-S-I-O-N." The lawyer stuck out his tongue and stamped his foot like a queen. "Who cares?" he said. "I don't care."

He turned and stomped off, leaving her in his office. Through the window she could see the courtyard. She watched the man who was trying to sell his sad story walk from the elevator and sit at the fountain. He had taken off his coat and had placed a hand in the streaming water.

"Isabel," Lucy said. She was standing in the doorway. She pointed at the phone. "Charles, please," she said. "He's called a gazillion times."

Isabel closed her eyes and tried to imagine what Charles would tell her. "I guess they finally found him," she said to no one.

Once she said it, it sounded real enough, and when she lifted her head, Lucy was still standing there.

"I know," Lucy said, walking into the room. She stood behind Isabel, placing a palm on her shoulder. Isabel tried to imagine picking up the phone but couldn't get her hand to move. Lucy picked up the phone and handed it to her.

"Isabel," Charles said.

He told her how warm it had been in Alaska this past spring. There was a long summer, and Billy was found buried headfirst, how frozen he had stayed the same, how his shoes had stayed on, and he was wearing the angel socks she had given him one Christmas.

She closed her eyes and listened. Charles was talking in the darkness, but she was floating around outside herself thinking about glaciers.

The air has shape, Isabel. Can you feel it?

"Hello?" Charles said on the phone. "Isabel. Are you listening? Did you hear what I said? They found Billy."

"I thought you said they found . . ." she said. They fell silent again and stayed that way, silent but breathing for what seemed to be a very long time.

"You need to make arrangements," he said.

Outside Isabel saw the gangster stare into space. He was removing his shoes, peeling his socks off, and he turned to place his feet in the water of the fountain.

"He was whole?" Isabel finally said. "Because he was frozen?"

There were choking sounds and a squeaking of Charles's sadness but no answer.

"Yes," Charles finally said. "He looks like he's sleeping."

And for a moment, before she felt consumed again, Isabel could see Billy so clearly.

Through the window, beyond the fountain, across the street at Thrifty she watched people walk in and out of the doors. Above them the late afternoon light poured over the rooftops in red beams. She stood and walked toward the window as if she was going to step through the glass but stopped. She then placed her hand on the cool glass and wished for things. She wished herself back to those long days of rain, big buckets of pouring-down fat rain, thinking if she stared through this window long enough she could make it happen even though she knew the truth of the matter. It was September in L.A. and the air was so hot it swirled off the desert like smoke. If she walked outside, she knew that she would feel its dry heat and be reminded again of Billy's breath on the edge of her skin. It made her sad to think of it, because she knew something then. Life would go on, but she would never know its beauty in the same way she had known it with Billy—swollen with possibility and as simple as making invisible boxes from air.

"Charles?" she said. "What do we do now?"

"We make arrangements, Is. We call his family and bring him home."

She was silent again. She was thinking about the words *we* and *home* and *fairy tale endings*. Here was the end to her story. Billy was frozen whole and she was moving forward in her life without him.

We the
Girly Girls
from Massachusetts

Of all the things people leave behind, a book of postcards to Caroline Kennedy wouldn't have seemed so strange if I had been certain that when Bonner floated to the bottom of the surfer's pool a year ago that she had intended to leave them for the world's eyes. Certainly, when I gathered them from her suitcase at the surfer's house and the boxes I found at her apartment in Santa Monica, I never saw them assembled into a book that looked like it had been made at Kinko's, sandwiched between two pieces of cardboard and bound with a wire spiral.

Over the last few months, since Bonner's mother has made the "Dear Caroline" cards available to friends and family, people have asked about them, wanting to know, for example, if the cards were real and, if so, when Bonner actually began them. Each time it's brought up I circle back to try to retrieve an acceptable answer, but I always come up short. It seems obvious that Bonner was too young in 1960 at the age of three to be writing Caroline postcards, but, as I've told the others, pinpointing the beginning seems less compelling than answering the question about why the cards might have continued for almost forty-odd years, each card unanswered, if ever sent, all of them copied by hand on old-fashioned cards and airmail letter paper, wrapped in Kleenex, and saved in wooden boxes along with half-eaten sandwiches covered and preserved in salt.

"For what?" I had asked her once. "Saved for what, precisely?"

"Art," she shrugged. "Art. And nothing. I guess."

Bonner stood behind me, unpacking an old egg crate she had brought along to show us. It was part of her new installation at a warehouse gallery space downtown. She lifted small wooden boxes full of rosebuds and swatches of old lace, a silver fork, a golden thimble, along with buttons and letters, and slowly placed each fragile object on the table. She handed me one of the cards, scrawled in a broken child's script on the back of a card with a drawing of two ponies.

Dear Caroline,
You have a pony named Macaroni. We have ponies, too.

She looked at me sadly and then wandered off into a flash of light.

In the living room later Lydia and Margs arranged and rearranged themselves on white couches in the hot midday light while in the kitchen Bonner danced eating low-fat double fudge pudding screaming "L.A. Woman" along with Jim Morrison. She danced alone to her reflection in her thong underwear, her little potbelly and her inch-long platinum hair, her tiny stick legs and perked-up breasts that stood still as she bounced. This was in November 1997, when we—Bonner, Lydia, Margs, and I—got together to celebrate our fortieth birthdays. We were staying in a Malibu beach house owned by Lydia's famous psychologist friend, the father of the primal scream. The house was spectacular in the way old Malibu houses often are. Trellises dripped with large pink and orange hibiscus flowers, and inside on walls the color of bone were black-and-white Helmut Newton photographs of famous people's asses that dotted themselves around a swimming pool like exotic shrubs.

This was only months after my husband, Jack, had left me for the PR woman and had moved to New York, and I felt as if I lived at the bottom of a well. For that week he was everywhere inside that ocean, and that ocean was everywhere inside that house; its sounds and smells floated in and out of doors like ghosts, and in the middle of all of it were these lovely old friends and, oddly, Caroline Kennedy. Everywhere we wandered through the bright bars and supermarkets of southern California we found her face plastered on the cover of magazines, on television specials, and on talk shows.

Dear Caroline,
We the girly girls from Massachusetts whose grandmoth-
ers hid cotton batons in the crème puffs. We the daughters of
the American Revolution who rode ponies and went to par-
ties. What lives we lead. By the dawn's early light! By amber
waves of grain! Drinking Cuba libres, smoking Virginia Slim
cigarettes, you on the cover of life, liberty, and good house-
keeping. You and your crooked Bouvier smile living your right
to privacy. We the girly girls from Massachusetts don't have
such problems. We lead unremarkable lives in Los Angeles,
San Francisco, Boston, and New York. We spend summers on
shores of all the shining seas eating low-fat Melba toast and
salami, wondering where the fucking horseradish is. We sit
across the tables from husbands and girlfriends, old friends
and new friends. We sit across the entire United States of
America in perfect anonymity, thinking shit, if Caroline
Kennedy just turned forty, that must mean we are forty, too.
Dear Caroline, how is it that our lives are half over?

It was unusually warm summer weather for November, and at night the moon hung outrageous and low and orange. Bonner ran through the waves in the warm buttery light. "She's crazy," Lydia said, kicking the sand. She walked a few circles around Margs and me. We were lying on our backs, watching the sky for intruders. "Aliens," Margs pointed. "Aliens!" I looked up in the sky and saw Venus.

"That's bonafiable," Lydia added. "Drugs or no drugs, she's out of her mind."

Lydia's a clinical psychologist; judgments are a way of life. I could barely see her face in the eerie light, but her freckles, her generous mouth, and her aristocratic Adams nose remained suspended in my mind as permanent fixtures.

"Either you get better," she said, "or you get worse."

In the distance, Bonner dove into the water. "Come on," she said. Her platinum head bobbed in between the white crests as I ran for her, taking off my sneakers, keeping my socks and sweats on as if to trick my mind into warmth. At first I waded a few feet, but it was too cold. I dove in and felt my heart skip a beat, the skin on my head instantly constricting from the icy water. A moment later, Margs surfaced, and we were bobbing on a trip to the adventurous old days when we, as teenagers, dove off an old train trestle into a reservoir and swam across to pull our bodies up the immense cement columns of the Massachusetts Turnpike Bridge. Breathless, we then shimmied along the outside of the guardrails, balanced ourselves in the center, and lifted our shirts over our faces to flash our breasts at truck drivers. When they slowed down we had to jump. *Jump, Margs. Jump!* And when we fell the fifty feet into the deep water, we practically died from laughter as we swam for our lives.

"It's not as cold as I thought," Margs said. Bonner dove under, and as I watched her vanish into the watery skin I felt nervous again. Even after ten years in L.A. it was still too trippy to be swimming in November. I rolled onto my back and looked to the sky and saw the moon, a cosmic smudge of luminescence, nearly full and casting enough light so that we swam in silhouette. Bonner popped up next to me, spitting water like a whale. "El Niño," she said. "I'm so sad about all the sea lions that will starve."

Margs did the butterfly, her arms swiftly cutting through the water. Her shoulders were swimmer's shoulders, strong and broad, but Bonner was too slight to carry such a stroke, and though she tried, she began to take on water, missing the rhythm of the up-

and-down and in-and-out, not able to coordinate the pumping action of her feet. I rolled in the water, resting finally on my back again, and exhaled, closing and opening my eyes, which were playing tricks on me in the night, the stars falling in streaks of white.

Lydia held up the latest version of *Good Housekeeping* with a picture of Caroline on the cover. "Can you believe this?" she asked. She then covered Caroline's eyes with two fingers. Above and below headlines blared: *Rose Kennedy's Irish Thanksgiving! Jackie's Holiday China!*

Bonner wasn't paying any attention. She was too busy trying to remember all the songs of *Hair*, but she kept getting mixed up with *Godspell*, which all mashed together in a strange seventies medley. "Day by day. We search for truth . . . Down to here. Down to where it stops by itself." She then exploded, her arms wheeling around her like the blades of a windmill. Her body suddenly stood straight as a board, and she raised her hand in a mock bugle, making a high-pitched *doodoodoodoo* before feigning static like a radio changing channels: *I want to be Jackie Onassis. I want to wear dark sunglasses.*

Afterward she sat in the bedroom, where there was the biggest TV I'd ever seen, with at least four million channels. "Turn it down," Lydia yelled, but the volume was too loud, so Lyddie had to get up and walk into the bedroom. I heard their voices and then the volume died.

Dear Caroline,
We search for truth to be self-evident. We search for your mother's pearls, long legs, and grace. Some of us find truth. Some of us wear Chanel, dye our hair, and get big jobs in the city.

One early evening Bonner and I lay on the floor and talked about truth. Bonner said she was the sort of girl who was confused by the truth.

"Confused by everything," she said. "Inside and outside. It's all a mess."

I didn't understand what she was saying. I was trying to pull a fire together, trying to remember all Jack's Eagle Scout tricks, but all I could remember was him shouting all the things Eagle Scouts were supposed to be: Loyal. Trustworthy. Reverent. Helpful. Courteous.

"Are you 'kay, guys?" Margs asked. She had just woken from a nap and was wearing that sleepy, creasy face, standing behind me with a blue-and-white plastic tub of no-fat Cool Whip, spooning the white fluff into her mouth. I turned on my heels and looked up at her. She hadn't changed a bit in the last twenty-five years. I turned back and blew on the fire. As it began to take hold we lay ourselves out on the floor. We tried to play Monopoly, but we were all too tired, plus it seemed ridiculous buying up Park Avenue.

"Think American! Murdoch, Fox-TV," Lydia said.

"No, he's not American," I told her. "Ted Turner. Satellites! Kennedy. Quaker Oats, General Electric, Wal-Mart, Microsoft."

Lydia sang a refrain from some stupid television show with Ava or Zsa-Zsa Gabor, nobody could remember.

"Who was arrested for beating somebody over the head with her pocketbook?" Margs asked. "Was that Zsa-Zsa?"

"It goes something like," Bonner said, "you can have the sheep, but . . . darling, give me Park Avenue."

We all looked at her. "Sheep?" Lydia asked, noticing but not saying anything until later that something was up with Bonner's eyes.

Dear Caroline,
Your family made money on bootleg liquor. Our families
lost theirs drinking it. Your father was president. Our fathers
were doctors, engineers, and lawyers. Your father said, Ask
not what your country can do for you but what you can do
for your country. Our fathers said, I wonder what the prob-

lem is with your mother. Your father said, I wonder what the problem is with Jacqueline. Our fathers said, Oh, how I loved that Marilyn; she was a peach of a girl. Your mother said, Here is the Blue Room. Our mothers said, Here is the purple room. Your mother said, Where is your father? Our mothers said, There are those who have and those who have not. Your mother said, Those who live and those who let live. You played football. We played capture the flag, and when we wrote you letters and sent along pieces of half-eaten sandwiches and samples of our ponies' hair, you never wrote us back.

When we were young, we rode our ponies up and down carriage paths under maple canopies. We wore jodhpurs and paddock boots, our hair in braids, freckles on our faces, stunned and entitled fair eyes, canary vests with brass fox buttons, and stock pins crafted of precious metals. Our fingers held beautifully hand-sewn leather braided reins, as our short little legs clutched the backs of fat ponies with names like Pepsi Cola, Huck Finn, Tar Heels, and Mary Poppins.

We all remember where we were the exact moment we heard the news when JFK was shot, but no one remembered anything about his election, except for Bonner, who even at three claims she remembered the precise moment, what she ate for lunch, the day of the week, as she remembered everything, including the number of hairs on the chin of her principal, the lace on the slip of her first-grade teacher who was so mean to her. She told us it was a Thursday, and Jack promised to fight for world freedom. In the newspaper that her mother saved, Jack and Joe, Rose and Jackie, all smiled for the cameras, though the mood was described as somber on account of the narrow margin. Kennedy, Bonner said, was tired and feeling sad because he stayed up late waiting for Nixon to admit he had lost.

Bonner's first letter, addressed to the White House, offered condolences about the president's tragedy, part of her lunch, a question about turncoats and redcoats, and finally the brilliant idea about offering all of our fathers. And then on instructions from our teachers we all sent postcards from a field trip to the Science Museum, where we had seen the Invisible Lady and eaten revolting quantities of Boston baked beans. We collected postcards of Bunker Hill, the tea party, and the statue of Paul Revere and wrote, "The Redcoats Are Coming! The Redcoats Are Coming!"

And, then . . .

We grew up, President Kennedy under the eternal flame, our fathers collecting *Road and Track* magazines. Her mother hung out with diamond dealers and shipping magnates. Our mothers entertained only themselves inside pretty clapboard houses surrounded by Crest-green-colored walls.

Years later, we rode our ponies alongside Caroline on fake fox hunts through Old Concord, but Bonner went to Harvard and said she saw Caroline everywhere at school. She even went as far as to spy on her. She had a friend who lived downstairs from Caroline's apartment in Somerville. Bonner sent a pair of jeans she claimed were Caroline's that she had lifted from their laundry room.

Dear Anna:
Guess who is at large at Harvard Yard. Regardez! Size 12 Lee Wranglers.
Love,
Secret Agent Bonner

In the morning I found Lydia and Margs standing on their heads in the middle of the living room. They had begun fancying themselves as Buddhists. The year before it had been Al-Anon for Lydia and Coda for Margs. They were busy being grateful all the time, something Bonner and I never understood. We sat in the kitchen all morning drinking espresso and smoking cigarettes and talked about our drug days. Our difference was that when I left drugs behind, Bonner carried them forward with her. She went down with them. She embraced them. She let them under her skin. She held out her arms for me to see. Dead veins with little blue tattoo scars up and down the underbelly of her arm.

I reached out, wanting to touch the dead spots of skin, because I understood the desire to be more than human.

Bonner said she thought she was an addict because she was stupid, because she spent her time obsessing about details that were irrelevant to others.

She told me that to keep her sanity in rehab in Venice she memorized all sorts of stuff—poems and declarations. "There is such poetry in early America," she said. "The founding fuckers! That among these rights are life, liberty, and the pursuit of happiness—that to secure these rights that governments are instituted among men. That whenever any Form of Government long established becomes destructive of these ends, it is the Right of the people to alter it or abolish, to institute new government, laying its foundation on such principles and organizing its powering such form, as to them shall seem most likely to effect their Safety and Happiness." She stopped.

"Isn't that fucking gorgeous?" she asked.

Then she told me about darkness and how the darkness in the world has to come out somewhere. "There is only so much the world can take before it begins to leak," she said. "That's where people like me come in—while evils are sufferable . . . that mankind is more disposed to suffer."

Bonner's face was the most amazing face—so small and fair with her porcelain skin and hazel eyes with those pools of yellow in the center. I watched as water collected and pools filled and I didn't know how to respond, because I began to cry, too, and she held me and sang one of our favorite songs from long ago, "Yesterday." Backward. The others joined in singing, making me laugh because they were such awful singers, all of them, but they continued to the end, shoulder to shoulder. "Squish!" they yelled and moved in, and as they did time stopped as if the calendar of days flipped backward instead of forward like in the movies, and I saw then that no matter how old we became, we would always live our lives as little girls.

After Lydia set off the house alarm the Malibu sheriff came and the rain began to fall in massive sheets. The police person, a Sergeant Porter, whom Bonner called Porker, stood in the kitchen and dripped water all over the famous psychologist's white floor and asked questions about security codes, which we didn't have.

While Lydia made calls to our host to track down the code, Margs and I watched Bonner flush her drugs down the toilet, what looked like an ounce of cocaine and maybe something else, whimpering, "You better not say a fucking word. I am dead if you say a word." Disgusted, Margs turned away and walked out, but I stayed and sat on the side of the kidney-shaped bathtub and looked at all the tiny blue tiles and thought about things that were sad and lonely—lost husbands, swirling drugs, abandoned cats, and old ladies.

In the afternoon we powered up our host's Jeep Cherokee and drove south on the beach road, where we found a fancy beach bar in which to pass the afternoon. The rain would continue for days, but that afternoon we watched the storm gather together and apart as the sea crashed in on us, the water's spray reaching the windows. On the other side of us there was a bar where there were four men and one woman. "All older, if that's possible," Lydia whispered. "They would be older." She leaned forward. "Shoot me, put me out of my misery if I ever look like that. Promise?"

She was referring to the older woman at the bar, midsixties, small and round like a beach ball who smoked Pall Malls nonstop as she kept pulling her shirt down in front with the hope of hiding her stomach, which had clearly gotten ahead of her. The music was loud and bad, but old surfer tunes were nostalgic nonetheless, so we moved in our seats. Margs cocked an ear, stood up, and looked at us, her face deadpan, her eyes closed.

"I love my body," she said. She wiggled a little and moved her hands up and down her stomach, over her breasts, to her neck, and down again. "I love my body. I do!"

We all began to howl. Clearly we had already been in this bar too long. Everyone was bombed. Even so we decided to stay until closing, approximately eight hours from that minute. Margs's *I love my body* sent us to the moon, because we all remembered the time as teenagers she stripped in dressing rooms all over suburban Boston and pretended to masturbate while stunned housewives looked on.

Margs began to strip, throwing off her sweater, and I sat back to pound bad coffee because I was already a little smashed and Bonner had just given me the end of her poem. "If I'm Paul Revere, you are John Hancock," she said, throwing a wad of napkins my way.

"The observer, the secretary of us four girls of Massachusetts. We the girly girls from Massachusetts, whose current goal is to pick a surfer boy, one for each."

Dear Caroline,
We the girly girls from Massachusetts, we lead lives we cannot forget. We lead lives and endure the consequences. We lead them and look back at them, knowing friends in need are friends indeed, sorrow falls on the heels of mirth, birds of a feather flock together, and in the end, silence gives consent.

Bonner then joined Lydia, who was squealing, wiping tears of laughter from her eyes, trying to recover from the sight of Margs sitting in her underwear.

"Paint a picture of us with words, Anna," Lydia said.

They mugged for me, leaning together on the other side of a wooden table, a wood of an unknown variety underneath many layers of varnish. On the left was Lydia, who wore a pink cashmere sweater, her elbows not on the table but on her lap, a swan neck with silky blonde hair at her shoulders. In the center was Margs, half-naked and the biggest of all. The lesbian minister. Tall and broad, with fire red hair and a hyena laugh. And then, at the other end, of course, our Bonner, the poet, holding her head in her hands, eyes closed, stoned on a mixture of martinis and cocaine.

"Smile," I said, and they threw their arms around each other's shoulders and stretched their mouths into shining testaments. Behind them the sun dipped in the West, making the sky a deep bruised purple with steely blue clouds that hung like mountains below. "Wave," I told them. They raised and waved their hands like beauty queens, laughing, and as they did, their faces froze still as if the memory caught like a piece of film in a movie projector. I half expected for the image to burn orange and bright, the years spinning halos of light around my head like tiny exploding flashbulbs.